You're a

Privileged

Woman.

Introducing
PAGES & PRIVILEGES™.

It's our way of thanking you for buying
our books at your favorite retail store.

GET ALL THIS FREE

WITH JUST ONE PROOF OF PURCHASE:

◆ **Hotel Discounts** up
to 60% at home and
abroad ◆ **Travel Service**
- Guaranteed lowest
published airfares
plus 5% cash back

$50 VALUE

on tickets ◆ **$25 Travel Voucher**

◆ **Sensuous Petite Parfumerie** collection

◆ **Insider Tips Letter**
with sneak previews
of upcoming books

*You'll get a FREE personal card, too.
It's your passport to all these benefits— and to
even more great gifts & benefits to come!*

There's no club to join. No purchase commitment. No obligation.

Enrollment Form

☐ *Yes!* I WANT TO BE A *Privileged Woman.*

Enclosed is one *PAGES & PRIVILEGES*™ Proof of Purchase from any Harlequin or Silhouette book currently for sale in stores (Proofs of Purchase are found on the back pages of books) and the store cash register receipt. Please enroll me in *PAGES & PRIVILEGES*™. Send my Welcome Kit and FREE Gifts -- and activate my FREE benefits -- immediately.

More great gifts and benefits to come like these luxurious Truly Lace and L'Effleur gift baskets.

NAME (please print)

ADDRESS   APT. NO

CITY   STATE   ZIP/POSTAL CODE

📖 **PROOF OF PURCHASE**
Pages & Privileges

Please allow 6-8 weeks for delivery. Quantities are limited. We reserve the right to substitute items. Enroll before October 31, 1995 and receive one full year of benefits.

**NO CLUB!
NO COMMITMENT!**
Just one purchase brings you great **Free Gifts** *and* **Benefits!**
(More details in back of this book.)

Name of store where this book was purchased_____

Date of purchase_____

Type of store:

☐ Bookstore   ☐ Supermarket   ☐ Drugstore

☐ Dept. or discount store (e.g. K-Mart or Walmart)

☐ Other (specify)_____

Which Harlequin or Silhouette series do you usually read?

📖 Pages & Privileges™

Complete and mail with one Proof of Purchase and store receipt to:

U.S.: *PAGES & PRIVILEGES*™, P.O. Box 1960, Danbury, CT 06813-1960

Canada: *PAGES & PRIVILEGES*™, 49-6A The Donway West, P.O. 813, North York, ON M3C 2E8   **PRINTED IN U.S.A**

> ## "As soon as you let me go, I'll call the police."

"Susan," Hunter said, shaking his head. "You wouldn't do that."

"Try me."

"I wouldn't call the police if I found you in *my* home."

His voice was softer now, much softer, and she felt the warmth of his breath brushing her cheek as he spoke. "What would you do?" she asked, knowing she shouldn't.

Hunter was watching her, his eyes glinting dangerously. "This is the only proper way to deal with an intruder like you."

His mouth closed over hers, fully and firmly, reminding her of other times and other places. It was almost as if he was claiming her as his. Again.

ABOUT THE AUTHOR

Before penning her first romance, Kay Wilding
was a copywriter for an advertising agency, a
free-lance writer and an editor for a trade-
magazine publisher. She lives in Atlanta,
Georgia, with her husband and their daughter
and son.

Kay loves books—all kinds, but especially
romances—crossword puzzles, her water-
aerobics class and movies that make her laugh
and/or cry.

Books by Kay Wilding

HARLEQUIN AMERICAN ROMANCE

Don't miss any of our special offers. Write to us at the
following address for information on our newest releases.

Harlequin Reader Service
U.S.: 3010 Walden Ave., P.O. Box 1325, Buffalo, NY 14269
Canadian: P.O. Box 609, Fort Erie, Ont. L2A 5X3

KAY WILDING

TOO MANY GROOMS

Harlequin Books

TORONTO • NEW YORK • LONDON
AMSTERDAM • PARIS • SYDNEY • HAMBURG
STOCKHOLM • ATHENS • TOKYO • MILAN
MADRID • WARSAW • BUDAPEST • AUCKLAND

For Nancy and Ted

ISBN 0-373-16595-1

TOO MANY GROOMS

Prologue

"I'm not going to die?" Hunter Townsend raised his eyebrows and stared in disbelief at the dapper little man in the white jacket.

"Not for at least fifty years or so," Dr. Chandler drawled. "That's my opinion. Of course, there's always the possibility of your being struck by lightning or drowning in the bathtub." He chuckled at his little joke. "But you're in excellent health."

"That can't be," Hunter said. "What about the brain tumor?"

"What brain tumor?"

"The damn brain tumor growing inside my head!" Hunter shouted, tapping his head with his index finger for emphasis.

Dr. Chandler gave Hunter a condescending smile. "The only thing growing inside your head is an overactive imagination. You certainly don't have a brain tumor."

"The doctor back in Atlanta said it was inoperable and that I'd be dead within a year," Hunter insisted. "I saw the X ray myself."

Dr. Chandler frowned. "How long ago was that?"

"Eighteen months. Are you saying that he gave me an incorrect diagnosis?"

"I most assuredly am *not* saying that," the doctor averred. "However, I do have one comment—you're still alive."

Hunter nodded. "But for how long?"

"Quite some time, as I told you before."

"So what happened to my brain tumor?"

"Maybe you lost it on the way to my office?"

The man was a frustrated stand-up comic, Hunter thought with annoyance. He considered the matter for a moment, then fixed the doctor with a steely stare. "You're lying."

Dr. Chandler bristled at that. "I beg your pardon."

"My tumor hasn't gone away at all. It's still there, ready to strike me down at any time. You're trying to make me feel better by saying it doesn't exist."

"No. Absolutely not. I'm saying that you don't have a tumor. As far as I can tell, you *never* had one. If you don't believe me, you can get a second opinion."

"Oh, sure. Like doctors are a dime a dozen down here at the edge of the biggest rain forest in South America."

The doctor shrugged.

"Besides," Hunter continued, "you *are* my second opinion. The other doctor told me I had an inoperable brain tumor."

"And I'm telling you that you don't have one now."

Good Lord, Hunter thought, slowly starting to believe in miracles—at least this particular miracle. Could it possibly be true? A year and a half ago, a lifetime ago, he'd thought he was dying. After much agonizing, he'd decided to live what little was left of his life going all out, full tilt. He'd dived for sunken treasure in shark-infested waters. He'd participated in a life-threatening Antarctic expedition. He'd lied about his credentials in order to be allowed to climb a mountain reserved only for the most experienced.

Hunter wiped away sweat that had suddenly broken out on his forehead. "I could have killed myself!" he said in horror as the realization dawned.

"Beg pardon?" Dr. Chandler asked.

Hunter ignored the question. "Then you are saying that the other doctor was wrong."

"No. I don't have access to his examination records and the reasons he might have made his diagnosis."

"Either he was wrong or you're wrong."

"Not necessarily. He may have thought he had valid reasons to suspect a tumor."

"He didn't say he was suspicious. He said he was positive."

"Well, sometimes X rays can be misleading."

Hunter was about to argue the point, but then remembered how doctors stuck together and none of them would say flat out that another one was wrong. More importantly, he suddenly recalled that the other doctor—the one who'd shattered Hunter's life by telling him he had an inoperable tumor with only a short time to live—had been recommended to him by Susan Willingham's stepfather.

Susan. For a year and a half, Hunter had tried to keep the memory of her buried a safe distance below the surface. For that entire time, he'd been unsuccessful. She was never far from his consciousness.

The two of them had been in love, engaged to be married. Susan's mother, quiet and charmingly gracious, hadn't voiced any objections to the marriage of her daughter to a struggling young man armed with a degree from Georgia Tech and not much else.

Susan's stepfather was another matter. Kenneth Brantley, ambitious and ruthless in augmenting the sizable banking interests he'd inherited, had made no secret of his disapproval of the match between Susan and Hunter.

"Damn!" Hunter said, thinking about Brantley. "I should have remembered that."

"You had no way of knowing how difficult it can be to interpret X rays," Dr. Chandler said soothingly. "Even if it looked—"

"Do you have a telephone I can use to call the States?" Hunter asked suddenly.

"Well," the doctor said, stalling.

"Don't worry about the cost," Hunter assured him. "The risks I've taken the past year have paid off. I have lots of money. Tons of money."

And none of it does me any good, Hunter thought dejectedly as he cradled the receiver for the final time hours later. From the maid, he'd learned that Susan was away, vacationing in Europe with her fiancé and his parents. After more calls, Hunter got Susan's stepfather on the line. Kenneth Brantley said yes, it was true that Susan was engaged to someone else, and no, there was no way she could be reached by phone, but that he'd tell her Hunter had been frantically trying to get in touch with her.

"And that's the end of that," Hunter said out loud as he hung up the receiver. He felt sure Brantley would never deliver his message. And even if he did, Hunter thought bitterly, there was no reason to believe that Susan would respond to it. After all, she obviously cared so little for him that she'd gone out and gotten herself engaged to someone else only a little more than a year after the two of them had planned to marry.

It was true that Hunter was the one who had originally walked away, but he'd felt guilty as sin for leaving Susan, and never would have done it if he hadn't thought he was dying. He'd had no doubt that Susan would have insisted on staying by his side if she knew about his illness, and he'd loved her enough not to ask it of her. He'd decided it would be better for her to hate him than for him to be a burden to her.

Dammit! He'd done a truly noble thing—sacrificed himself in order to spare her!

And had Susan been moved by his gesture? Had she been heartbroken? Hell, no! She'd forgotten all about him a little more than a year later. Damn her, anyway!

Feeling worse than he'd ever felt in his life—in spite of his new lease on it—Hunter said goodbye to Dr. Chandler. Even though he now had a future, he didn't know what to do with it.

Chapter One

"I think I'm going to be sick," Susan Willingham announced.

"Oh, no!" one of her bridesmaids shrieked.

"Bend over and hold your head between your legs," another bridesmaid said. "Or is that what you're supposed to do when you feel faint?"

"I'll get you a wet towel," a third bridesmaid offered. "But you'll need to be careful not to muss your makeup."

"Could someone please hand me a glass of water?" Susan croaked.

"How about a slug of bourbon?" one of them suggested. "It worked for me. I can't even remember walking down the aisle."

"I'll bet you remember being wheeled into the delivery room nine months later, though," still another bridesmaid countered.

Everybody laughed.

Everybody except Susan, who groaned. "I really am going to be sick."

"You'll do no such thing," her mother said calmly. "It's only bridal jitters. Take a couple of deep breaths."

Susan complied, and did feel marginally better.

"I think I need to have a short one-on-one with my daughter," Helen Willingham Brantley said, flashing a conspiratorial smile at the assembled bridesmaids. "It will only take a moment, and I'm sure you understand."

Even feeling as ill as she did, Susan had to admire her mother in action. She was a work of art, oozing tact and charming each bridesmaid in turn as she gently but firmly directed them out the door of the dressing room.

After closing the door behind the last bridesmaid, Helen Brantley turned her solemn, unsmiling face to Susan and fixed her with a steady stare. "You don't have to go through with this, you know."

"Mother!"

"I mean it. If you don't want to get married, then don't. I'll cover for you."

Susan shook her head. "All those people. There must be hundreds by now." The ceremony was only minutes away and through the solid oak door leading down a short hallway to the church foyer, she had been hearing the sounds of people arriving for almost an hour. "What would you say to them?"

"I'll think of something."

Susan managed a vestige of a smile. "I'm sure you would. But I couldn't ask that of you. I wouldn't."

"You don't have to ask me. I've already volunteered."

"And I appreciate it. I . . . I appreciate you." Susan swallowed. "But I'm feeling better now. Like you said before, it's probably a case of bridal jitters."

"I said that for the benefit of the others," Helen stated firmly. "But I think it's something much more than that."

Susan shook her head. "No."

"I think it's all tied in with what happened two years ago."

"No!"

"Susan." Helen crossed the room and took Susan's cold, clammy hands in hers. "I'm your mother. I'm on your side. You can talk honestly with me."

"There's nothing to talk about! What happened two years ago is over...done. I've forgotten it."

"Honestly?" Helen asked gently, squeezing Susan's hands. "You've actually forgotten that Hunter Townsend jilted you and left you standing at the altar?"

Susan winced and withdrew her hands. "It wasn't at the altar. He disappeared a couple of days before the wedding."

"A technicality. The fact remains that the two of you were in love. At least, you were. I've never seen anyone more in love than you were, Susan. You positively glowed. And you were shattered when Hunter suddenly dropped out of sight without a word. He didn't even bother writing you a note."

"Please, Mother. I'd rather not talk about it."

"I'd rather not talk about it, either. That's why we *haven't* talked about it for two long years. I think it's past time we brought it out in the open at last."

Susan sighed. "What good will that do?"

Helen sighed, too. "I have no idea. Except maybe it will prevent you from making the same mistake you almost made with that other fellow. You know the one. He was your second fiancé, that polo player you became engaged to after Hunter dumped you. What was his name?''

Susan winced again and wished her mother had saved a little of her abundant tact and charm to use on her daughter during this discussion. But no. Helen was in one of her rare call-it-like-it-is moods. "Giorgio," she said. "And what mistake was that?''

"Marrying a man you don't love.''

Ouch. "I didn't marry Giorgio," she countered defensively.

"No," Helen agreed. "You came to your senses in time and called it off. Maybe you should do the same thing now.''

"This is different." Susan clenched her fists and willed herself to believe what she was telling her mother. She had become engaged to Giorgio on the rebound, only a few months after Hunter disappeared. *Correction.* It was after Hunter *jilted* her. At Helen's insistence, the family had hired detectives to search him out discreetly, to make sure he was still alive.

The detectives found him, to be sure, living it up in the Florida Keys. He was in marvelous health and happy as a lark, the detectives reported. He was even diving for sunken treasure! Susan recalled her reaction in vivid detail—relief that he was alive, then shock, and finally fury. *Damn Hunter Townsend to hell!*

In retaliation, Susan had allowed herself to be swept off her feet by Giorgio, but only for a short time. And now, finally—two years after Hunter left her—she was once again in charge of her mind and emotions.

"Michael is different, too," Susan said, managing a smile for her mother's benefit. "He's no Giorgio.''

"That's for sure," Helen agreed. "Giorgio was a rogue and a Romeo, but at least he had a little fire to him, the same way Hunter did. And he was almost as handsome as Hunter."

Susan wondered briefly whose side her mother was on. "Michael is handsome," she protested.

"Pleasant," her mother corrected.

"And Michael has fire, too. He can be romantic."

"Do his kisses make your toes curl the way Hunter's did?"

"Will you forget about Hunter!" Susan snapped.

"The point is," Helen said, "have *you* forgotten him?"

"Yes! Almost," she amended. "Most of the time."

"That's what I thought," Helen said sadly, shaking her head. "You haven't forgotten him at all."

"Have you forgotten my father?" Susan shouted, feeling the need to lash out. She was immediately sorry for her outburst and watched with chagrin as her mother seemed to crumple before her eyes.

"No," Helen said softly. "I haven't forgotten him at all, either. When he died, the best part of me died with him."

"I'm sorry, Mother. I shouldn't have said that."

"I probably shouldn't have married your stepfather," Helen continued, ignoring Susan's apology. "Kenneth Brantley can be a bit pompous and overbearing at times, and I knew that full well when I married him. At the time, I thought the trade-off was worth it. He's a handsome, charming man and I thought we suited each other very well. I admit I was wrong."

"Mother—"

"I thought I'd found what I needed in Kenneth. But even so, a woman's needs are different at my age than they are at yours, Susan. You're only twenty-six, for heaven's sake! You have a whole life ahead of you."

"I know that! I didn't agree to marry Michael because I was desperate. I've had plenty of male friends, as you well know."

Helen nodded. "I know."

"Then what's your point?"

"Michael is the antithesis of Hunter."

"So?"

"Don't let the Hunter thing cause you to go through with a marriage to the wrong man."

Susan took a deep breath. "I'm not." She hoped—prayed—that was true. "Michael is kind. Gentle."

"So's your Aunt Louise," Helen said, not unkindly.

"Mother."

"Sorry. I couldn't resist."

"It's true that he isn't a skyrocket in flight, the way Hunter was," Susan admitted. "But I don't think I could live with that anymore. I want peace and serenity. Security. Someone I can grow old with."

"You'll have all that with Michael," Helen agreed. "I'd say that the two of you will be old folks together before you're thirty."

"Mother!"

"But if that's what you really want..."

"It is."

Helen shrugged. "Then go ahead and throw up. After you finish, I'll call the bridesmaids back in so we can get on with the ceremony."

Susan laughed. "I think what I really wanted and needed was to talk with you like this."

"Hmm."

"I mean it." Susan hesitated. "I love you very much, you know."

"I love you very much, too. But what does that have to do with the price of apples and oranges?"

"Everything."

"I just hope you're doing the right thing."

"I am," Susan stated emphatically. She stood up and straightened her shoulders. *I am,* she repeated to herself. She'd worked hard to get her life on track again and finally it was. *She* was. "And I'm not going to be sick. What I am going to do is march down that aisle, marry Michael Verner and live happily ever after."

HAPPILY EVER AFTER. Susan kept repeating the phrase to herself as her bridesmaids fussed over her, applying last-minute finishing touches—adding a tad more eye shadow to accentuate her green eyes, loosening a couple of dark chestnut curls to give her upswept hairdo a more romantic look and adjusting and readjusting the bridal veil until Susan finally said, "Enough."

Happily ever after. At last, Susan stood beside her tall, handsome, distinguished stepfather with her arm looped through his. She listened to the sounds of the wedding processional echoing through the cathedral while she watched her bridesmaids—her treasured longtime friends—sedately make their way down the familiar aisle of St. Phillip's.

Happily ever after. Susan tried valiantly to push aside a nagging memory that simply wouldn't go away. It was the recurring memory of a lost dream, a dream she'd envisioned so many times that it almost seemed to be a reality—her marriage to Hunter Townsend. It would have taken place here, in this special and magnificent cathedral, on just such a day as this.

Oh, Hunter, what went wrong? Why did you run off and leave me the way you did? Do you know how much you hurt me? How could you be so cruel? It wasn't like you to be cruel. It wasn't like you at all.

Happily ever after. Susan's stepfather squeezed her hand. She blinked, looked down the aisle and saw that all the bridesmaids had completed their passage and were now assembled at the altar. The organist was sounding the opening chords of the wedding march. Susan swallowed.

"You look absolutely lovely," Kenneth Brantley said, giving her hand another squeeze. "So much like your mother."

Susan tried to murmur something, but her voice wouldn't work. She finally managed a smile and hoped that would suffice.

Her stepfather returned the smile. "Shall we be on our way then?"

Susan nodded.

They started walking. Slowly. In small, measured steps. The altar seemed two miles away, give or take an inch or so.

Susan's breathing was shallow. Her heart pounded furiously. She was sure that the guests filling the cathedral on both sides of the aisle could hear the pounding and the panting. She tried to smile, but it came out one-sided—silly-looking, she was sure—so she abandoned the attempt.

Her heart continued pounding. Was that the reason all these people were staring at her?

No, silly, she told herself. *They're looking at the bride. You've done it yourself a hundred times. A thousand times. "Here Comes the Bride" and all that. It's the reason they're here. It's the reason you're here. Happily ever after.*

Somewhere along the way, Susan forced herself to look at Michael standing beside the altar. *No, that can't be correct,* she thought. She hadn't *forced* herself to look at him. Her eyes must have hungrily and eagerly sought him out. Yes. That's what had happened.

And there he was. Yep. That was Michael, all right. The formal gray cutaway he wore was unfamiliar, but other than that, she'd have known him anywhere, immaculately groomed sandy hair, gray eyes and all. *Pleasant*-looking, her mother had said. Her mother was right.

There was nothing dashing or daring or incendiary about Michael. But he was a nice man. Quiet. Controlled. *Exactly what I want,* Susan told herself.

Susan's eyes met Michael's. She smiled. He smiled. Yes. There would be no more skyrockets in flight for her, and no trips to the moon on gossamer wings, either. She'd had enough of that sort of thing, more than enough to last a lifetime. Now that she was finally grown-up, Michael was precisely what she wanted, what she needed.

Happily ever after. So there.

Susan and her stepfather continued down the aisle, getting closer to the altar and Michael by the moment, with each measured step they took in accompaniment to the organist's crescendos. *Happily ever after,* Susan reminded herself when she was close enough to see the whites of Michael's eyes. *And don't you forget it.*

Finally arriving at the altar, Susan's gaze met that of the minister who would perform the ceremony, her longtime friend Nancy Wages. They'd been in nursery school together, and in kindergarten and grade school. They had lost touch for a time when they attended different high schools and colleges, and Susan had been thrilled when Nancy returned to St. Phillip's, as a minister, no less! And now, her childhood friend would be performing her marriage ceremony, a perfect touch.

Mounting the last steps, Susan took her place beside Michael, the man with whom she would be spending the rest of her life. Michael smiled at her. Nancy smiled at both of them.

Then Susan's attention was distracted by a movement she barely perceived out of the corner of her eye. Turning her head, she saw a tall, dark, tuxedo-clad man emerge from the anteroom and boldly approach the altar. She heard a gasp and didn't know whether the sound came from someone in the audience or from her own lips.

The man was nearing the altar, coming closer with each long stride he took. His deeply tanned face was so determined that it could have been carved of stone. His eyes were as dark as his hair and seemed to flash fire.

Susan tried to speak and couldn't. "No," she finally managed to whisper.

"Susan?" Michael asked, concern shading his voice.

"Susan?" Nancy repeated. "What is it?"

The tall, dark, tuxedo-clad man arrived at the altar. With a grim smile, he gently but firmly moved the best man aside and took his place beside Michael.

"What are you doing?" Michael said indignantly. "You can't come in here and—"

"I just did," the man replied in a deep baritone.

"Who are you?" Nancy Wages asked.

"Why are you here?" Michael asked.

"I'm Hunter Townsend," the man replied calmly. "And I'm here to get married. I'm the groom."

Nancy's mouth fell open.

Michael gaped.

Susan fainted.

Chapter Two

Hunter Townsend watched silently while everybody else in the church seemed to go crazy. Bridesmaids shrieked and screamed. Groomsmen dashed to and fro. The bride's stepfather and the guy in the gray cutaway—evidently the groom—worked frantically to revive her.

They finally succeeded. Susan's eyes fluttered several times and opened. She looked around wildly before her gaze eventually settled on him. She promptly closed her eyes again.

"Damn it all, Townsend," her stepfather grumbled. "Can't you at least have the good grace to get out of Susan's line of vision until we have a chance to revive her?"

Susan opened her eyes again. "I'm revived," she said distinctly, glaring at Hunter. "What are you doing here?"

Hunter smiled. "Hello, Susan."

Susan didn't smile. "I repeat. What the hell are you doing here?"

Hunter kept his smile in place. "Like I said before, I'm here to get married. To you."

"Susan, who *is* this man?" the gray cutaway asked.

She struggled to sit up. "He's—"

"The name's Townsend," Hunter interrupted. "And who are you?"

"He's Michael Verner," Susan replied, rising to her feet.

She was getting ready to do battle, too, Hunter noted with satisfaction when he saw the fire in her green eyes. *Good.* He had been acutely disappointed when she fainted at her first sight of him, because he was ready to do battle himself. More than ready.

When he had first learned of her perfidy six months ago, he'd decided to forget her and get on with his life. But then, when his sister had sent him the news clipping about Susan's big fancy wedding, he'd changed his mind. Knowing how much Susan hated scenes, he'd decided to make a big one.

His pulse quickened as he waited for her assault.

"Michael is my fiancé," Susan stated emphatically. "He's the man I'm going to marry."

Hunter pretended shock. "Susan!"

"And we'd like to complete the ceremony today, if it's at all possible," she continued, appearing totally unmoved.

"What about me?" Hunter asked.

Susan narrowed her eyes. "What *about* you?"

"You're engaged to marry me, too."

"That was two years ago!"

"Even so—"

"And you're the one who didn't show up for our wedding!"

"I had reasons."

"Where have you been for two years?"

"It's a long story. Can we go someplace and talk in private?"

"We most certainly cannot! I'm right in the middle of my wedding, for heaven's sake!"

"That's not precisely true," he told her. "The ceremony hasn't started yet."

"It *will* start... just as soon as you go back to wherever you came from and crawl back under your rock."

"Not before we talk," Hunter insisted.

"We have nothing to discuss."

"There are things I need to explain to you."

"You have nothing to say that I want to hear," Susan said, her green eyes flashing fury. "The time for explaining was two years ago. Instead, you walked off without a word. You sneaked away in the night, like the snake you are."

"Dammit! You have to hear me out. You owe it to me. To us."

"I don't owe you a damn thing!"

"Susan." Hunter reached out his hand.

She jumped away. "Don't touch me!"

"I wasn't—" Hunter stopped midsentence when he felt a heavy hand on his shoulder, whirling him around. His mouth dropped open with surprise when he saw Michael Verner's fist headed directly at his face. He tried to lift his arms to protect himself, but it was too late. He heard the sound of bone making contact with flesh. His flesh. His jaw.

Hunter staggered backward, but didn't fall down. He heard someone in the audience scream.

"Michael!" Susan exclaimed.

Hunter rubbed his jaw. "Why'd you do that?" he asked Verner.

"You were threatening my fiancée," Michael responded.

"She's my fiancée, too," Hunter told him.

"Stop saying that!" Susan said.

"And I haven't threatened anybody." Hunter took a menacing step toward Verner. "But I might change my mind."

Verner stood his ground. "Anytime you're ready."

"Stop it, you two! *Now!*" Kenneth Brantley ordered. He glared at Hunter. "I suggest that you leave before you cause us any further embarrassment."

Hunter shifted his attention to Susan's stepfather, and narrowed his eyes in speculation. If his suspicions were correct, this was only the beginning of the embarrassment he intended to cause Kenneth Brantley. However, now wasn't the time to go into that. "I'm not leaving until I talk with my fiancée," he said.

"I told you to stop calling me that!" Susan cried.

"So it *is* you," a feminine voice behind Hunter said. "I thought it was, but couldn't be sure from where I was sitting."

Turning, Hunter saw Susan's mother coming up to join the assemblage at the altar. He smiled. "Hello, Mrs. Brantley. It's nice to see you again."

"Thank you, Hunter." She returned his smile. "What brings you to Atlanta?"

"I came for the wedding."

"Oh." She paused for a moment, then frowned. "Susan and Michael's wedding?"

"No. Susan's and mine."

"Are you crazy?" Susan exclaimed. "That's ridiculous!"

Hunter ignored Susan and kept his eyes trained on her mother.

"Really?" Mrs. Brantley said. "You're a trifle . . . tardy, wouldn't you say?"

Hunter laughed. "Better late than never."

"I suppose," Susan's mother agreed, laughing with him. "Still, two years *is* a long time. What happened? Did you have amnesia or something?"

Hunter lifted his eyebrows. "How did you guess?"

"Amnesia!" Kenneth Brantley exclaimed.

"Amnesia," Michael Verner repeated.

"Amnesia?" Susan said. "You're lying!"

"Susan," Hunter admonished, shaking his head. "That's not a very nice thing to say."

"And what happened to this so-called amnesia of yours?" Susan asked. "Did you wake up one day and suddenly find it gone?"

"It's possible," the minister said. "I've read of cases where that happens."

Hunter flashed her a grateful grin.

"So have I," Mrs. Brantley added.

"Mother! Surely you don't believe Hunter's outrageous fabrication."

"I didn't say that," Mrs. Brantley retorted. "But I didn't say that I disbelieve it, either."

"Mother!"

"I'm just trying to be fair."

Susan frowned. "Whose side are you on, anyway?"

"Yours, dear," Mrs. Brantley responded immediately. "But suppose for a moment—just suppose—that Hunter is telling the truth."

"What?"

"Suppose he really did have amnesia, and miraculously recovered."

Susan opened her mouth to speak, then closed it again. She finally sighed. "Okay. I'm supposing. Now what?"

"My point exactly," Mrs. Brantley said.

"What do you mean?"

"I mean, what happens now?" her mother replied. "The shock of seeing his former fiancée marry someone else could set Hunter off again. It could cause his amnesia to come back. Would you want his relapse on your conscience?"

"You're not even sure he *had* amnesia," Susan said, feeling that she'd fallen into a rabbit hole and had to fight her way out. "What makes you think he'd have a relapse?"

Mrs. Brantley stood her ground. "You'll have to admit it's a possibility."

"What are you leading up to, Mother?"

"Would you like to postpone the wedding, Susan?"

"Absolutely not," Kenneth Brantley said.

"Yes! By all means," Hunter said.

"No, by thunder!" Michael Verner said.

"Susan?" Mrs. Brantley asked her daughter again.

Susan shook her head. "I'm so confused now, I can't even think straight. What do you suggest, Nancy?"

The minister considered the question for a long moment. "Under the circumstances, it might be wise to wait. It'll give everyone time to sort things out."

"Susan, surely you're not—"

"That makes sense to me," Mrs. Brantley said, cutting Michael off in midsentence.

"What do we tell all these people?" Kenneth asked.

"The truth," Hunter said. "That the wedding has been postponed."

"You stay out of this," Susan warned him.

"I'll make a brief announcement," Mrs. Brantley volunteered. "And then I'll explain that the reception will take place as scheduled."

"We can't go on with the reception!" Susan exclaimed in horror.

"We most certainly can!" her mother stated firmly. "Anything else would be out of the question. These people are our guests. It would be unforgivably rude of us to cancel the reception in *addition* to the wedding. And it's already paid for, too. Of course we'll go ahead with it!"

EXCEPT FOR the absence of a receiving line, it was almost identical to every other wedding reception Susan had attended at the Piedmont Driving Club through the years. Lavish but tasteful decor and decorations. Magnificent food. Impeccable service. Drinks aplenty. Smooth, danceable music provided by the current rage among society orchestras. And beautiful, well-dressed people. Hungry people. Thirsty people. Dancing people. Laughing people.

Susan laughed and drank and danced along with the rest of them, but carefully avoided getting anywhere close to food. Her stomach was tied in knots. She still hadn't recovered from the shock of having Hunter turn up again after two years.

It didn't help that everyone she talked with made the same observations, asked the same questions. Hunter was *so-o-o* handsome. Why had he jilted her two years ago? Was it really true that he'd suffered amnesia? Was she planning to dump Michael and run away with Hunter now? Wasn't it all *so-o-o* romantic?

Hunter was lying through his teeth about the amnesia, of course. Susan had promised her mother not to make a big scene during the reception, though, so she fended off all questions pertaining to his so-called loss of memory. She tried to ignore Hunter, as well, but it wasn't easy. The more she fended him off, the more insistent he became.

Like now. Over the shoulder of her current dance partner, Chaz Martin, Susan spied Hunter purposefully making his way across the floor. He was coming to claim her again. He'd already danced with her so many times that Michael was furious. She didn't blame Michael. She was furious, too, and was about to renege on her promise not to make a scene.

"Sorry, old buddy," Hunter said, tapping Chaz on the shoulder to cut in.

"You're no friend of mine," Chaz muttered under his breath.

"Your loss," Hunter replied cheerfully as he slipped his arm around Susan's waist and whirled her away. "Glad to see me?" he asked her.

She hated it that her heart started beating faster at that very moment. "I'd hoped that you were gone by now," she replied in an even voice.

Hunter merely laughed, a deep familiar baritone sound that immediately conjured up unwanted memories of other times, other places. He'd always laughed easily. And often. She'd always loved his laugh.

The memories his laughter evoked were fragmented, in no particular order. There was a house party at a beach on a remote island with several other couples whose names she couldn't remember. What she did remember was standing beside Hunter on the beach at sunset. He was tall and deeply tanned, even more so than he was now, and the offshore breeze tousled his dark hair. She'd stolen glances at him, thinking he was the most gorgeous man she'd ever seen. He was serious, solemn even, but then he'd laughed and she knew for the first time that she was in love with him.

There was the memory of sitting through a football game in a driving rainstorm. Hunter had bought a couple of ponchos for the two of them, but the glue that held the ponchos together began to disintegrate during the first quarter. Susan and Hunter sat through the rest of the game laughing at each other as they watched the glue melt and run onto their clothes.

Going further back, Susan recalled a debutante party the year she'd come out—the first time they met—when Hunter had been recruited from the Georgia Tech campus as an extra escort simply because he had a tuxedo. "And it wasn't even mine," he explained to her later, laughing at the memory. "My ex-roomie forgot to take it with him when he graduated, and I was too broke to ship it to him."

She remembered the time she'd had to have an emergency appendectomy. Hunter was in the middle of final exams at Georgia Tech, but as soon as he learned about her surgery, he'd skipped his last exam, borrowed a friend's car and driven all night, arriving at her bedside in New Haven a little before dawn. She'd been so moved, so elated, so relieved and so happy to see him that she'd burst into tears. He'd comforted her, then teased her, and the tears had turned into laughter. Soon both of them were laughing, and the harder they tried to stop, the worse it got. By the time a muscular orderly evicted Hunter from her room, Susan was laughing so hard that she was in danger of breaking her stitches.

"Why are you smiling?" Hunter asked, bringing Susan back to the present.

"I wasn't smiling."

"It was a happy smile," he insisted. "As if you were remembering something pleasant."

"I can't imagine what that could be," she lied. "This hasn't exactly been a red-letter day for me."

"It could have been worse. You could have actually married Mr. Gray Cutaway."

"I still *am* going to marry him."

"Why?"

"Because I love him, of course."

Hunter shook his head. "I find that hard to believe."

"Believe what you want. I *am* going to marry him."

He shook his head again. "You deserve much more than a gray cutaway, Susan."

"Damn you!" She took a deep breath, furious with herself because she'd let him get to her. "His name is Michael. Michael Verner. He's a . . . a lovely man."

"Where did you meet him?"

She took another deep breath. "As a matter of fact, I met him through Kenneth."

"Your stepfather?" Hunter raised an eyebrow, considering that information a moment before nodding his head. "It figures. Kenneth Brantley always hated my guts, and only tolerated me because of you and your mother. So he decided to pick your fiancé himself this time."

Susan felt her cheeks grow warm. "You're completely off base, as usual. Kenneth merely introduced us at a big party. Michael and I were attracted to each other at first sight and had a whirlwind romance. We became engaged a short time later." That was the lie of the century but she felt secure in telling it because Hunter had no way of knowing the truth.

"What kind of party was it?"

His abrupt shift caught her off guard. "What do you mean?"

"I mean was the party where you met Michael a big social occasion at the driving club? The harvest ball? What?"

Oh, hell, she thought. *Leave it to Hunter to pick up on something like that.* "It was a party in Ponte Vedra."

"What was the occasion?"

"A bankers' convention," she replied quickly, almost whispering the words.

"Ah-ha!" he said triumphantly.

"What's that supposed to mean?"

"Your Prince Charming in the gray cutaway—the one who swept you off your feet—is a *banker!*"

"You have no right to say that!"

"That he's a banker?"

"It was your tone of voice." Her own voice was high-pitched and she was perilously close to losing control. "I'll have you know that Michael *is* charming. Romantic, too. And his family owns one of the oldest, most prestigious banks in Switzerland."

"Whew." Hunter whistled under his breath. "I'm impressed. I'll bet old K.B. is, too."

Susan glared at him, not bothering to reply. They danced in silence, and she gradually calmed enough to notice the song the band was playing. It was "When I Fall In Love," and it had been *their* song, hers and Hunter's. She remembered a night years ago when they'd played it on a jukebox at a bar somewhere. They'd danced to it a dozen times or more, holding each other tightly, loving each other completely. Her throat tightened.

Hunter tightened his arm around her waist now, pulling her closer. "Recognize that song?" he whispered in her ear.

She wanted to lie, but couldn't bring herself to do it. She nodded instead, wanting to cry.

Hunter lifted his head to look at her, his dark eyes boring into hers. "Do you and Michael have a special song?"

"That's no concern of yours."

"But it *is* my concern. You and I are still engaged."

"What?"

"Nobody broke the engagement. I know I didn't."

"You don't consider walking away—disappearing for two years—to be breaking an engagement?"

"Not if there's a good reason."

"Ah, yes," she said. "Your amnesia."

"That's right. And no words were retracted, no ring was returned."

"I didn't know where to send your damn ring."

Hunter grinned. "You kept it? Good."

"I'll return it to you by messenger tomorrow. Tonight."

"The ring is yours, Susan. I don't want it back."

"I don't want it, either. I—" She stopped when she saw Michael looming over Hunter's shoulder, coming to claim her. Thank goodness.

Hunter didn't relinquish her immediately. He kept his arm around her waist and continued gazing into her eyes as if he didn't ever want to let her go. Susan tried to look away, tried to break the spell, but couldn't seem to summon up enough energy to do it.

She felt strangely lethargic. The strain of all that had happened today must have caught up with her.

With a sigh, Hunter finally stepped back. The place on her waist where his hand had been suddenly felt cold as ice. "Take good care of her," he said to Michael.

"I intend to," Michael replied. "In the meantime, why don't you go back to wherever you came from."

Susan frowned. Where *had* Hunter come from? Where had he been these past two years? What had he been doing? There were so many questions she hadn't asked him.

"I hope he'll take the hint and leave," Michael said, drawing Susan into his arms.

"Leave?" she repeated. Hunter couldn't leave, not now, when there were still so many unanswered questions. She looked around and didn't see Hunter. *Take good care of her,* he'd said to Michael. Maybe he *had* left, gone out of her life forever this time. She tried to tell herself it was good riddance, but she felt frustrated, irritated. The two of them still had unfinished business.

Michael pulled her closer, and they were dancing cheek-to-cheek. Susan sighed and tightened her arms around his neck, but something was just not there. Her mother was right, she realized. Michael was no Hunter. But she should be happy about that, not sad, not feeling that she was missing out on something important.

What was wrong with her? Michael was a really, really nice man, so the problem must be with her. Had Hunter spoiled her for any other man, or spoiled any other man for her? Susan closed her eyes. She was getting a headache. Too much thinking. Too much booze. Too little food.

A man she'd never seen before cut in on them. Before she had a chance to ask the man his name, though, Hunter was back to claim her once more. "I remembered the debutante rules," he announced proudly. "Never cut directly back in on the guy who cut in on you. There has to be an intermediate partner. Right?"

Susan laughed. She wouldn't allow herself to examine the reason she was happy beyond belief to be with him again. She only knew she was. "Something like that," she said.

The band segued into "When I Fall In Love." Again. Susan looked at Hunter and lifted an eyebrow. "How did that happen?"

"Guess."

"You shouldn't have done it."

"Why not? Nobody knows it's our song, except the two of us."

"That's the point. *We know.* I know."

"It brings back old memories, doesn't it?"

"They're memories I'd rather forget."

"Not me," Hunter stated emphatically. "I'm happy as a lark to have memories again after all this time."

Susan narrowed her eyes to look at him. "When did your memory come back?"

"Several weeks ago."

"If you still believed the two of us were engaged—and that's a big if—why did you wait until today to contact me?"

"My memory didn't come back all at once, just bits and pieces at a time."

He was slippery as an eel. She'd thought she had him that time, but he'd managed to escape her trap. She tried a new tack. "Did you start getting headaches again?"

"Headaches?"

"Don't you remember the headaches you started having a few weeks before the date of our wedding?"

"Oh, yes. *Those* headaches."

"Right. After you disappeared, I thought about them a lot," Susan said slowly, choosing her words with care. "I finally decided that they might have been stress headaches. And I thought they might have been brought on because you didn't want to be married to me."

"No," Hunter said, shaking his head. "That's not true." He looked directly into her eyes. "At that time, I wanted to be married to you more than anything in the world."

And now? she wondered. "Tell the truth, Hunter," she said. "You never really had amnesia, did you?"

"Why are you so anxious to condemn me?"

"You didn't answer my question."

"I have no intention of dignifying it with an answer." Hunter took a deep breath, then tilted his head to one side to look around her. "Uh-oh."

"What?"

"I see your Prince Charming heading this way."

"Good."

"You and I still have a lot to discuss," he told her.

"I thought we'd just about covered everything."

"Don't you even want to know where I've been all these years? What I've been doing?"

Of course she did. And of course he knew she did. "Not particularly," she lied.

"There are tons of things I want to ask you," he said. "Have lunch with me tomorrow?"

"No," she replied automatically.

"You have other plans?"

"I *had* planned to be flying off to St. Croix on my honeymoon tomorrow. Remember?"

If she'd hoped to make him feel contrite, she realized a moment later that she'd failed miserably.

"Well, since that's been scrubbed, why not have lunch with me?" he said cheerfully. "We'll have time to talk, and I can answer all the questions you've been dying to ask me."

Susan couldn't believe that she would agree to have lunch with Hunter, after all the pain and heartbreak—not to mention the humiliation—he had caused her. But she did.

Chapter Three

From his seat by the restaurant window, Hunter saw Susan drive up in a red BMW convertible. The weather was warm for March, even by Atlanta standards, and she'd left the top down. He watched as she removed a bright red polka-dot scarf from her hair and rearranged it around her neck.

Her shoulder-length hair was loose today, rather than upswept the way it had been yesterday when she was a breathtakingly beautiful bride. He watched as she ran her fingers through her hair, pushed her sunglasses higher on her nose, then opened the car door and got out. It was typically Susan that she never bothered looking in a mirror.

The loose-fitting, navy knit dress she wore was sedate, but too softly clingy to be prim. Hunter caught a glimpse of a nylon-clad feminine thigh before she stepped to the ground and pulled the hem of her skirt down. He sighed.

She was even more appealing than he'd remembered.

Hunter hadn't expected that. He'd expected her to have changed, of course, but not for the better. He'd somehow thought that her past actions would have branded her, making her face hard, her voice brittle. He'd thought that her callousness would be evident in the way she looked, walked, talked,

But that wasn't the case. By all appearances, she could have been the same sweet innocent that he'd believed her to be when he fell in love with her years ago. He'd have to guard against repeating that particular mistake. Falling in love with her again could spoil his chances of finding out what really happened two years ago... and of getting even.

Hunter narrowed his eyes while he watched Susan approach the restaurant. When he'd disrupted her wedding yesterday, he'd merely been intent on embarrassing Susan and her stepfather. He'd intended to leave immediately afterward.

It was Susan's mother who'd come up with the suggestion that he'd had amnesia, and he'd gone along with the idea. Now he looked on the amnesia as a godsend. He could use it to help him reestablish a relationship with Susan. Then he could use her to help him find out exactly who did what to turn his life upside down two years ago.

He was almost certain that Kenneth Brantley was involved up to his ears and eyeballs. But what about Wayne Estep, the doctor recommended by Brantley? Would a doctor deliberately make a wrong diagnosis? Or had he been instructed—possibly coerced—into falsely insisting that Hunter had a brain tumor?

Still another possibility was that Dr. Estep had made an honest error. But if so, shouldn't it have been discovered? Didn't they double-check life-and-death pronouncements such as the one Hunter had received?

Last—but perhaps most important of all—how much did Susan know?

Hunter intended to find answers. And if they were what he expected them to be, he'd confront Kenneth Brantley. There might not be a law against what that bastard had done, but Hunter would at least expose him to the world.

He would have to be careful. Susan already suspected that his claim of amnesia was a lie. She had no way of knowing for sure, though…not unless he told her. And that was something he had no intention of doing.

Hunter pushed back his chair and stood waiting for Susan while the maître d' escorted her to the table. "I wasn't sure you'd actually come," Hunter said as soon as they were both seated.

"Neither was I," Susan admitted. "It was still up for grabs at the last minute."

"I'm glad you decided to do it. Are you?"

"Mmm," she replied noncommittally. "We'll see."

"Would you like a glass of wine? Or a cocktail?"

She shuddered. "Thanks, but no thanks. I drank enough yesterday to pickle a cucumber."

"Celebrating your narrow escape, huh?" he suggested.

Susan was still wearing her sunglasses, and lifted them with one manicured finger. "I have a splitting headache, Townsend. And you're treading on dangerous ground." She lowered the glasses.

"Sorry. How about something to eat?"

"The way I feel, that's a little iffy, too. Maybe I can manage a cup of hot tea and a croissant."

"That sounds vedy, vedy European to me," Hunter said in an exaggerated accent. "Is it Herr Verner's recipe for a hangover?"

"Or maybe I should leave right now," Susan said, starting to get up.

Hunter's hand shot out to clasp her wrist and pull her back down. "I'm sorry. It was a bad joke."

"Very bad."

"Vedy, vedy bad," he agreed.

Susan snickered.

"That's a good sign," Hunter said, gesturing for the waiter. He ordered Susan's tea and croissant, and the brunch buffet for himself. "I'm not hungry, either. Two or three trips through the buffet line should do it for me."

She smiled then, and removed the sunglasses, placing them on the table.

Hunter, feeling encouraged, plowed ahead. "All I really wanted today was to be with you."

"Hunter..."

"Merely to talk," he added hastily. "To fill in all the blank spaces. What's going on in your life now, Susan? Besides Michael Verner, of course."

"If you invited me here to pick a fight..."

He held up his hands. "Not guilty. I already know about your Prince Charming. Tell me something I don't know."

"For instance?"

"Anything. Such as...what do you do with your time when you're not walking down the aisle at St. Phillip's?"

"I work."

"Volunteer work?"

"That, too. But I also work for money. I'm an art director at one of the top advertising agencies in town." She named the agency with a certain degree of pride.

Hunter whistled. "Congratulations."

"Are you being sarcastic?"

"No. I mean it. Really."

"But... ?"

"I'm a little surprised that you're, uh, involved in commercial art," he said, being truthful. "As opposed to 'real art,' as you used to call it."

Susan rolled her eyes. "I was a sappy schoolgirl back in those days. And for your information, advertising *is* real art. The field attracts some of the brightest and best talents around."

"I didn't say it didn't. I merely said I was surprised that it attracted *you,*" Hunter insisted, warming to the argument as he suddenly recalled some of their heated discussions that would go on for hours. Hunter had never met anyone he loved to argue with as much as he did Susan. They were perfectly matched. It was one of the things he loved most about her.

Used to love most, he corrected himself.

"And you were never a sappy schoolgirl," Hunter added. "You were a talented, intelligent idealist... unwilling to march to anybody's drumbeat but your own."

"I made the decision to enter advertising on my own," Susan responded hotly. "My family had nothing to do with it. And they never pulled any strings to open doors for me."

Good Lord, Hunter thought, wondering when she had become so defensive. "I never thought they did."

"And I *was* sappy back in those days," she insisted.

"Why do you keep saying that?"

"I became engaged to you, didn't I?"

Hunter frowned, taken aback by her vehemence. Judging by her attitude, he wasn't the only one with a score to settle. He took a deep breath, refusing to allow himself to sympathize with her point of view. She'd just have to stand in line if she wanted to punish him for the past. His grievance took precedence.

"Was that such a terrible mistake?" he asked quietly.

"Maybe not by your standards," she replied. "But up until then, it was the worst one I ever made."

"And since then?"

She shrugged. "I've made a few. I think our engagement still tops the list."

That was a depressing thought. *If she really meant it.*

Hunter decided to test her on it. One of her hands was resting on the table between them. He reached out and covered it with his. She looked up at him, her eyes widening with surprise.

"I'm sorry you feel that way," he said slowly, watching her closely for a reaction. "I thought our engagement was the best thing that ever happened to me. I had hoped it was the same for you."

His little test produced a reaction, all right, and it was almost Hunter's undoing. Susan blushed furiously, then almost immediately turned ghostly pale. She pulled away from his grasp, and he saw her hand tremble as she brought her water glass to her lips to take a sip.

The depth of her emotion came as a shock to him. Of course, she could be acting, but if she was, she deserved the Academy Award for it. Hunter had a sudden impulse to jump from his seat, pull her into his arms and kiss her until they were both senseless. Luckily, he had wits enough to know that she'd probably bop him if he attempted such a thing. He remained frozen in his seat, waiting for her to make the next move.

She took a deep breath. "Why did you do it, Hunter?"

He saw the cold fury in her eyes, replacing the vulnerability that had been there only moments ago.

"Why did you *really* run away and leave me standing at the altar two years ago?"

Did she really not know that he'd left in order to spare her pain? Was she acting now? Hunter narrowed his eyes. "Why did you become engaged to someone else?"

"It happened two years later, for God's sake!"

"I'm not talking about your engagement to Verner. I'm talking about the other one...the one that happened only a few months after you and I were supposed to be married."

"So I was right about your flimsy excuse of amnesia, all along!"

"Don't try to change the subject," Hunter insisted.

"You never had amnesia, did you?"

"Of course I had amnesia."

"Then how did you know about that other engagement of mine?" Susan announced triumphantly. "How do you explain that?"

"When I recovered and came back here a few weeks ago, my sister showed me the newspaper clippings that she'd saved at the time."

Susan frowned. "Why did she do that?"

"Because she loved me, and because she knew I... cared about you. And because, unlike you, she never believed that I'd run off like a thief in the night. She always assumed that something bad must have happened to me."

"So did I!" Susan whispered fiercely. "Until I discovered that you were not only alive and well, but also happy as a lark, living it up in the Florida Keys," she added bitterly.

"What?" Susan or her family must have hired private detectives. Hunter wondered what else she might have discovered about him.

"That's right. The detectives my mother insisted on hiring found you right away."

"Why didn't they confront me? Why didn't *you* confront me, once you knew where I was?" Hunter asked, attacking because that was the first rule of a good defense.

"I didn't *want* to confront you!" Susan said. "I knew you were okay, and that you'd deliberately run off and left me. What else was there to say?"

Hunter's heart was pounding fiercely. *Take it easy,* he told himself. "You might have asked me to come back home with you," he finally said.

"And if I had asked you that," Susan persisted, looking him directly in the eyes, "what would your answer have been?"

She had him there. At the time, he'd thought he was dying. Hunter shook his head. "I have no idea."

They stared at each other in silence for a long moment. Susan looked away first. Then the waiter brought her food and Hunter excused himself in order to go through the buffet line. When he returned to their table, she had a bright, false smile firmly in place. "Good afternoon, Hunter," she said pleasantly.

He frowned. "What's going on?"

"I thought we could start this meeting over again. Maybe we can do better this time around."

"Sounds like a good idea to me," he agreed.

"And just to set the record straight about my being engaged that other time... It only lasted a few weeks."

"What happened?"

"I called it off. And I told him in person," she added pointedly, then lifted her teacup with a steady hand and took a sip.

"Why did you break the engagement?" Hunter asked.

She gave him a look that said it was none of his business.

He thought about pressing the point but decided against it. He shrugged.

"What have you been doing these past couple of years, Hunter?"

"Well..." He scratched his chin. "You already know I was in the Florida Keys for a time. I was with a group diving on a sunken ship looking for lost treasure."

She snickered. "You're kidding."

"I'm completely serious. That lasted about six months."

"You gave up?"

"We found the treasure."

She raised her eyebrows. "Do tell."

"After that, I joined an expedition to the Antarctic."

"My goodness. Why on earth did you do that?"

"It seemed like a good idea at the time. And they paid me a nice sum of money. Unfortunately, I had to spend most of it recovering from frostbite afterward."

"I never knew you were such an adventurer."

"Neither did I."

"Is that why you..." Susan stopped in midsentence.

"Why what?" he asked, knowing she was wondering if that was why he'd left her at the altar.

"Never mind."

Hunter paused a long moment. "I recouped the money I lost on the Antarctic trip, and much more, when I helped uncover an extraordinary cache of jewels in a remote mountain region of South America."

Susan was eyeing him with suspicion now, and Hunter didn't blame her. His stories sounded so farfetched that he wouldn't have believed them himself.

"Are you pulling my leg?" she asked.

He was fully prepared for the question. "I have pictures," he said, producing an envelope containing a carefully selected dozen or so photographs of himself taken on various adventures.

Susan handled the photos as if they might be contaminated, but carefully examined each in turn. "Is this really you?" she asked, pointing to a shot of him in Antarctica.

"Underneath all that hair?" he asked with a laugh.
"Yes. A beard isn't considered an affectation in that
cold climate. It's a necessity."

She thumbed through a couple more photos, then
held up a particularly revealing one of him made
aboard the dive boat in the Keys. He was deeply
tanned and clad in a bathing suit that could best be
described as "European brief," meaning it covered
almost nothing. "I suppose this was a necessity, too,"
she commented.

Hunter laughed. "Not a necessity, but extremely
comfortable in scorching hot weather."

"Hmm." She gave the photo one last look, then
quickly went on to another. When she'd seen the
batch, she handed them back to him, shaking her
head. "Treasure ships, the Antarctic, South America, the Mediterranean...you've certainly been busy."

"I didn't actually set out to have an adventure,"
Hunter said, remembering the bleakness of those early
days when he thought he was dying, and recalling his
conscious decision not to waste a single precious remaining moment. "It was just something to pass the
time."

"Well, you surely did that." She hesitated. "I
imagine, by comparison, marriage would have been a
deadly bore."

"You can't believe that's why I went away!" Hunter
said.

"Can't I?"

"It's not true."

"Be honest, Hunter."

"I am. It's simply not true. I loved you."

"Perhaps you did. But even so, you'll have to admit that you hated the career my family—especially my stepfather—was trying to force upon you."

Hunter hesitated. "I agree that banking was never my number-one career choice."

"You detested every minute of it. You were meant to be a designer and a builder, for heaven's sake. It's what you trained for, worked toward for years.... That's why I pleaded with you not to accept Kenneth's offer to work at the bank."

"It was a lot of money, Susan. Enough for us to get married."

"That didn't matter to me."

"It mattered to me!" he insisted.

"Not in the end, it didn't. You walked away from the job as easily as you walked away from me."

"That's not..." Hunter had begun hotly, but caught himself in the nick of time, before he said too much. "I had amnesia," he finished lamely.

Susan's green eyes flashed warning signs. "How stupid of me to forget," she said after an eternity.

Hunter sighed. "Shall I go outside and then come in once more, so we can start our meeting a third time?"

"I really need to be going soon," she said, glancing at her watch.

"But you just got here!"

"It was almost an hour ago, Hunter. And I promised to meet Michael later on."

"Why?"

"Because he's my fiancé, that's why!"

"So am I."

"Don't start that again, Hunter."

"But..."

"Besides, Michael and I have important things to discuss."

"So do you and I," Hunter insisted.

"I think we've already covered most of—"

"No! There's still so much I haven't asked you...about your mother, for instance."

"You saw her yourself just yesterday," Susan said wearily. "She's much the same as usual."

"And your stepfather...?"

"*You* want to know about Kenneth?" she asked incredulously. "Surely your amnesia hasn't made you forget how much you dislike the man."

"Well...I know you think he's been good to you," Hunter said, hedging. "There must be something about him I missed, because I know you care about him, and your mother positively dotes on him."

"What?"

"Don't you remember? You and I used to laugh because the two of them carried on like a couple of teenage newlyweds."

"Hmm," Susan said. "That's not true anymore."

"No?"

"Mother divorced Kenneth several months ago."

Hunter was dumbfounded. "But...why? How?"

"Don't ask me. Neither of them would tell me anything except that they were getting a divorce."

"But yesterday... He was giving you away," Hunter stammered.

"Even if he's no longer married to my mother, Kenneth is still my stepfather."

Hunter tried to digest this latest information, to put it into some sort of perspective with what he already knew or suspected about Brantley. But it didn't compute. He plowed ahead, anyway. "How is his health?"

Hunter knew that question, out of the blue, made no sense at all. He was grateful to Susan for bothering to reply.

"Fine," she said with a frown. "You saw him just yesterday, too. Remember?"

"Does he still go to that same doctor?" Hunter asked, finally getting around to the nitty-gritty.

Susan sighed. "He goes to half a dozen doctors. And a couple of dentists, as well."

Hunter nodded. "I forgot that everyone sees specialists these days. A doctor for the left toenails and a different doctor for the right toenails, correct?"

"Which doctor did you have in mind?" Susan asked.

"I was thinking about Dr. Estep, the one that Brantley suggested I go to see."

"You?"

"He treated me for the headaches. Remember?"

"Oh, yes. I'd forgotten about him," Susan said.

"He's a, uh, fine doctor. Don't you think?"

"I have no idea. I've never met him. My stepfather changes doctors the way some people change shirts."

"Oh."

"I suppose I could find out if Kenneth still sees him," she added. "Is it important?"

"Oh, no. I was just curious."

"What did Dr. Estep say about your headaches, by the way?"

"Nothing much," Hunter said, hedging, undecided about how much to tell her.

"He didn't find out what was causing them?"

"Not exactly."

Susan frowned. "There's something you're not telling me, Hunter."

He took a deep breath. "The thing is...I wasn't having headaches—not seriously, anyway—until your stepfather insisted that I go to Dr. Estep for a check-up."

Chapter Four

For a long moment, Susan stared at Hunter in disbelief. "What are you saying?" she finally asked.

"If you remember two years ago," Hunter said, "your stepfather insisted that I have a physical before our wedding."

Susan shook her head. "As I recall it, he *suggested* that you have one, since you hadn't been to a doctor in years."

"Whatever. Brantley suggested it, and recommended Dr. Estep."

"That was because you didn't have a doctor of your own."

"Okay," Hunter agreed with a sigh. "So I went to see Estep, who poked and prodded and couldn't find anything wrong with me. He kept asking about ailments I'd had in the past and I kept telling him I hadn't had any. He seemed so disheartened that I finally felt sorry for him and mentioned a couple of sinus headaches I'd had the previous spring."

"So?" Susan asked, wondering where this monologue was headed.

"Estep immediately pounced on that bit of information, as if I'd just handed him a treasure. He gave me some sample tablets and wrote out a prescription for more.''

"What kind of tablets were they?" she asked.

"I'm not sure—antihistamine, I thought at the time. I never had the prescription filled, but I started taking the tablets Dr. Estep had given me. And almost immediately, I started having severe headaches. Surely you remember them.''

"Of course I remember," she replied irritably. "And I remember we argued about them. I thought the headaches were caused by stress and that you should see a therapist.''

"And I told you that I had no intention of seeing a shrink," Hunter said.

"After which I told you that was a totally unreasonable attitude.''

"Right," he agreed.

"So now you're saying that you think the tablets themselves might have caused the headaches?''

"I'm saying it's a possibility.''

Susan shook her head. "You're way off base.''

"Why?''

"It's too farfetched.''

"I repeat—why?''

"Any doctor worth his salt would know what side effects—if any—a certain medication would produce. He'd warn you about them. And he wouldn't deliberately give you something to make you ill.''

"He wouldn't?" Hunter asked pointedly.

Susan gasped. "Are you saying you think Dr. Estep *did* try to make you ill?" She shook her head. "He had no reason to do that.''

"Maybe it wasn't his idea.''

"What?" She blinked. "If it wasn't his idea...then whose was it?"

Hunter's gaze met hers, but he didn't reply. Slowly, the significance of what he was saying, and not saying, dawned on her.

"No!" she stated emphatically.

"No what?" Hunter asked.

"Don't make innuendos and then try to play innocent with me, Hunter Townsend. If you're suggesting that my stepfather deliberately set you up by referring you to a quack who fed you pills to induce terrible headaches...then..." She stopped only because she'd run out of breath.

"Then what?" Hunter prompted.

"Then say so!"

"Okay, I'm saying so."

"That's preposterous!"

"I knew you'd say that, but think about it a minute—"

"I don't need to think about it," she interrupted.

"Kenneth Brantley never wanted you to marry me," Hunter stated emphatically.

"He showed you every courtesy," Susan told him.

"He had his mind made up even before he met me. He actually accused me of being a fortune hunter."

"At least he said it to your face. He didn't go behind your back..."

"The way I'm doing now? Is that what you mean?"

"If the shoe fits..."

"Dammit, Susan, the man did everything he could to sabotage our relationship."

"Does your definition of 'sabotage' include offering you a cushy job as assistant vice president at the bank?"

"He only did that for your benefit!"

"Of course he did it for my benefit...*and* for yours."

"He did it because he expected me to fail."

Susan rolled her eyes. "So when you didn't fail—when you succeeded beyond anyone's expectations—Kenneth had to roll out plan B, is that it? He had to convince a perfectly respectable doctor to go against the medical oath he'd taken, and deliberately set out to poison you. Is that what you're saying?"

"I didn't use the word *poison*," Hunter protested.

"Why not, pray tell? You've accused him of everything else."

"Maybe I overstated the situation just a little..."

"Yes," Susan said, getting to her feet. "I'd have to agree with that. Definitely."

Hunter scrambled out of his chair and put a restraining hand on Susan's arm. "Listen..."

She shook off his hand. "I've heard quite enough."

"But—"

"You may or may not have had amnesia, Hunter. But I still suggest, very strongly, that you see a therapist."

He opened his mouth to speak but she raced out of the restaurant before he could get the words out. Hunter watched until she was out of sight, then sat back down in his chair.

"Damn!" he muttered. He'd known he was going too fast, throwing too much at her all at once. But the years of frustration and resentment had finally caused him to reach the boiling point and explode. Then, voicing his suspicions to Susan and seeing her disbelief, he'd said more than he intended. Actually, he wasn't at all sure that the pills Dr. Estep gave him had caused his headaches.

Susan was correct in pointing out that he'd been under a lot of stress, but was wrong to think the stress had had anything to do with her, except indirectly. Working at the bank, Hunter had become suspicious of some loan practices there. He had nothing concrete to support his suspicions, nothing he could prove and nobody he could tell. He was willing to concede that his headaches could have been brought on by that situation, but he wouldn't budge on his conviction that Kenneth Brantley had something to do with Dr. Estep's false diagnosis of an incurable brain tumor. After today, he was going to have a hard time convincing Susan of that, though.

Hunter sighed. That didn't mean he was giving up on her. Far from it. In spite of what she'd said, her actions today had indicated that she wasn't immune to him, not by a long shot. Of course, the opposite side to *that* coin was that he wasn't immune to her, either. He would have to be both cautious and daring in dealing with her. And a bit of luck wouldn't hurt.

He smiled as he considered the possibilities.

"LATE AGAIN," Susan said under her breath as she pulled into a parking space close to the rear entrance of St. Phillip's. She was supposed to have met Michael at Nancy Wages's office at half past three, but lunch with Hunter had lasted longer than she'd anticipated. On exiting the restaurant, she'd found that the springlike weather of the morning had taken a nasty turn. Clouds had rolled in and the temperature was much colder, so she'd taken time to raise the top of her convertible before leaving the parking lot.

After that, she'd somehow managed to catch a red light at every single intersection on the drive across town.

The lunch itself had been every bit as unsettling as she'd expected it to be. When she'd first caught sight of Hunter in the restaurant—dressed casually in slacks and a blazer, but still managing to exude enough sexual magnetism to attract the attention of every female in sight—her first impulse had been to hightail it out of there as fast as she could.

She should have followed her impulse.

If she had, maybe she wouldn't have made such an absolute idiot of herself. She wouldn't have ranted on about their engagement being the worst mistake she'd ever made... and then blushed and stammered like a schoolgirl when he'd touched her and said the engagement had been the best thing that had ever happened to him. He was just being polite, for heaven's sake! She'd practically forced him into a corner and he'd *had* to say something.

She cringed, too, as she remembered practically drooling over the photograph of Hunter in a skimpy bathing suit that didn't so much conceal his masculinity as call attention to it. In her defense, he *was* a magnificent specimen, and the photo was more provocative than a completely nude one would have been. But still...she should have exercised more self-control even though she'd kept it to herself. And she certainly shouldn't have compared the photograph in her hands with her mental picture of Michael!

And while she was on the subject of Michael, what on earth was she going to say to him and Nancy at this meeting? She'd fully expected to be able to tell them that she'd discovered Hunter's claim of amnesia was a fraud and that they could go ahead and reschedule the wedding as soon as possible.

That's what she had expected. Now, she wasn't quite so certain. Hunter's farfetched accusations about her stepfather and Dr. Estep had caused her to have serious doubts. It seemed entirely possible to her—even likely—that a person who'd only recently recovered from something as traumatic as amnesia would still feel shaky and insecure, and thus would be overly suspicious, perhaps to the extent of being paranoid. That theory, if correct, could explain Hunter's wild ideas about the doctor and Kenneth Brantley, whom Hunter had never liked in the first place.

Susan shivered when a blast of arctic air hit her as soon as she got out of her car. Hunching her shoulders, she raced up the steps of the church and headed down a corridor leading to Nancy's office. She had been so sure that Hunter's claim of amnesia was a lie. Now she wasn't sure about anything, especially her own emotions.

Knocking on the door to Nancy's office, Susan entered without waiting for a reply. Nancy and Michael were seated side by side on the sofa and both jumped to their feet simultaneously. If Susan hadn't known better, she would have thought they were embarrassed about something. Nancy rushed over to give Susan a warm hug. Michael followed and gave her a light peck on the cheek.

Susan couldn't help noticing that her friend's greeting was warmer than her fiancé's. But then, Nancy had always been effusive, whereas Michael had always been reserved. In addition, Michael was still sulking about the wedding being called off yesterday. Susan didn't exactly blame him for that, but did think he could try to be a bit more understanding. She wondered if he knew how unattractive sulking could be in a man.

"You're late," Michael said, stating the obvious.

"Yes. Sorry," Susan answered, looking at Nancy.

"It's okay," Nancy replied with a grin. "Michael's been filling me in on what you've been up to these last years."

"Uh-oh."

"Not to worry," Nancy said. "He was extravagantly complimentary. Your bribe must have worked."

"It was money well spent," Susan agreed with a laugh. She noticed that Michael wore a puzzled expression, and explained, "It's a running joke Nancy and I started when we were kids. Instead of bobbing for apples, we'd play bribing for compliments."

She could tell that Michael still didn't understand, but she wasn't in the mood to explain further. She was grateful when Nancy interrupted by offering tea. "Yes, thank you," Susan said.

"Well, how did your meeting go with that man?" Michael asked, walking across the room to take a seat in a wing chair.

Susan wondered why he didn't sit on the sofa next to Nancy, where he'd been before she arrived. It irritated her to think that he might think she was petty enough to object. His supercilious tone of voice irritated her even more.

"That man?" Susan repeated pointedly. "Do you mean Hunter, the man I once planned to marry and spend the rest of my life with? That man?"

Michael flushed a bright red.

Nancy, ever the diplomat, stepped in again. "Of course he meant Hunter. Were you able to decide whether he was telling the truth about having amnesia?''

Susan shook her head. "No."

"He never had amnesia," Michael stated. "Even before your meeting, you were almost sure he was lying."

"But what if I was wrong?" Susan said. "What if Hunter really did have amnesia, after all?"

"What if he did?" Michael repeated. "I can't see that it makes much difference whether he did or not."

Susan caught her breath. *Oh, but it does make a difference,* she thought. *It makes all the difference in the world.*

"You were skeptical yesterday," Nancy said. "Did Hunter say something to make you change your mind?"

"I haven't exactly changed my mind. It's just...I'm less sure than I was yesterday."

"Why?" Nancy asked.

Susan thought about Hunter's dangerous exploits, and the foolhardy chances he'd taken. She thought about his strong accusations concerning her stepfather and Dr. Estep. She considered sharing her misgivings about Hunter's state of mind with Nancy and Michael, but immediately discarded the idea. In spite of her anger toward Hunter after what he'd done to her, she wouldn't betray his confidence.

She shrugged. "It's a feeling I have—woman's intuition, I suppose."

"And what about our wedding plans?" Michael asked. "Even if the man did have amnesia, it's nothing to do with us. I think we should go ahead and reschedule the ceremony as soon as possible, either tomorrow or the next day."

"Not if you want me to do the honors," Nancy said. "My calendar is full until the middle of next week."

Michael looked at Susan. "What about...?"

"Nancy and nobody else performs my wedding ceremony. Period."

"Of course," Michael agreed. "I was merely going to suggest we go ahead and book her for next week, while we can."

Susan didn't for a minute believe Michael's obvious lie, but went along with it, anyway. She gave him her brightest, sweetest smile. "We'll set it up as soon as we can. We only need to be patient for a little while longer, darling."

"Does your so-called woman's intuition tell you exactly how long that is?" he asked.

"I don't know," Susan replied evenly, her smile slipping a bit. "But I'm sure things will eventually work out exactly the way we want them."

AFTER AN EARLY DINNER with Michael, Susan drove to her house in Morningside. He had wanted to follow her, and had hinted at spending the night, but she had pleaded exhaustion. Then, feeling guilty because she'd been so snappish with him all evening, she invited him to come over for breakfast the next morning. It was a move she already regretted, because she would like nothing better than to sleep late and then putter around her own domain with her own thoughts.

Oh, well. She'd probably be happy to see Michael again in the morning after a good night's rest.

As soon as she turned into her driveway, Susan sensed that something was wrong. It wasn't until she pulled under the porte cochere beside her house and killed the engine that she figured out what it was.

The light outside her front door was glowing brightly.

The light had to be turned on from a switch in the hallway, *inside* the house.

Susan hadn't turned on the light, because she'd left the house early this morning in broad daylight.

The only two people with keys to her house were Michael, whom she'd just left, and her mother, who would never ever simply drop in for a visit with anybody, not even her own daughter.

Which meant...somebody else was inside her house. Or had been.

Susan took a deep breath. Morningside was an older, established neighborhood, quiet and relatively crime-free. She had never heard of a break-in on her street in the year she'd lived here. Dammit. Why did hers have to be the first one?

And what should she do? Start the car again and drive someplace to call the police? That was the sensible thing. But Susan wasn't feeling particularly sensible at the moment. She was tired, on edge...and angry. Mad as hell, in fact.

Acting quickly before she could change her mind, she got out of the car and quietly closed the door behind her. Instead of going up the stairs to the front porch as she usually did, she moved to the side of the house and cautiously made her way toward the back. She was shivering violently—either from the cold, excitement or fright, possibly all three—but she was determined.

Halfway there, she saw a light in the kitchen.

Whoever had broken in was probably still inside the house!

Oddly, that realization made her calmer, angrier and more determined to oust the intruder herself. But she would need a weapon. An ax or a sledgehammer would be nice, except she didn't own either.

Susan nodded with satisfaction when she remembered the garden tools she kept stored in the crawl space under the back porch. She should be able to subdue the intruder with a hoe or spade. After that, she could tie him up with the clothesline she kept strung across one end of the porch.

As soon as she reached the side of the porch, Susan dropped to her knees and peered underneath. It was starting to rain now, and was so dark she couldn't see a thing. She stretched out one hand, then the other, feeling around and trying to locate a tool. She came up empty. Moving closer, she hit her head on an overhead support.

"Ouch!" she muttered without thinking. She clamped a hand over her mouth and stayed still, not breathing, for a long moment. She finally relaxed when she didn't hear anything.

Lying down on her stomach this time, she started to crawl under the porch but stopped almost immediately when she felt a cobweb on her face. Shuddering, she wiped it away, then extended one hand to brush away any others that might be lingering.

At last, she inched forward again, feeling her way with one hand, then the other, and trying not to think about what sort of creepy-crawly creatures her hands might encounter. "Ah!" she breathed with satisfaction when she finally felt the smooth wooden handle of a garden tool.

She lifted it a tad, then moved it from side to side a bit while she tried to figure out which particular tool she held. She couldn't tell what it was, but then she found another tool with her other hand and decided to bring both of them out with her.

She started inching backward. Progress was slow and difficult. The tools kept getting tangled up with each other, and one of them caught on something else. She didn't know what it was, possibly a porch support, but she kept shifting and pulling until she finally had the tool free.

Muttering under her breath, she resumed her backward progress. She was almost out from under the porch when suddenly, out of nowhere and without a sound, something or somebody grabbed her right ankle.

"What—" She tried to twist around to see what was going on. She bumped her head again. Then her left ankle was caught in a viselike grip, as well, and she felt herself being pulled out from under the porch.

It must be the intruder! Too startled to scream, Susan tried to dig in, but her opponent was too strong. She did manage to hold on to the garden tools while she was forcefully removed from under her own back porch.

When she was finally out in the open, Susan felt the man's hands move from her ankles to her shoulders. She was sure he was getting ready to turn her onto her back and she was ready for him. More than ready.

As soon as he applied pressure to her shoulder, she rolled all the way over, bringing up the garden tool in her right hand as she did so. The handle was too long for her to land a proper blow, but the impact was enough to send him backward.

"Hey!" he yelled.

Susan lifted her hand to deliver another blow, but before she could move, the man was on top of her, smothering the breath out of her. She relinquished her grip on the garden tools and fought him hand to hand, hitting whatever she could, scratching, kicking, clawing . . . and even managing to bite him once.

"Damn!" he cursed when her teeth sank into his shoulder. He tightened his arms around her then, and rolled both of them over and over on the grass until she was finally forced to relinquish the teeth-hold she had on him.

It was pouring rain now, and Susan felt herself tiring. The man finally captured both her wrists in his hands, holding her arms above her head in an iron clasp. Both of them were panting.

They faced each other only inches apart for the first time.

"You!" she exclaimed, seeing Hunter's flushed face and flashing black eyes looking down at her.

"You!" he echoed. "What the hell are you doing here?"

"I live here!" she shrieked. "How did you get inside my house? Did you break a window or—"

"Certainly not. I used a key."

"You're lying. You don't have a key!" she said hotly.

"Your mother loaned me her key."

"My mother?" Susan moved her head, wincing when she felt a sharp pain in her shoulder. "Why did she do that?"

Instead of answering her question, he muttered an expletive. "I could have hurt you badly. Why were you crawling around under your porch at night?"

"I was looking for a weapon."

"A weapon?" he repeated. "A garden hoe?"

"Yes," she replied huffily. She was increasingly conscious of his body lying atop hers—not covering her completely enough to make her unable to breathe, but enough to make her breathless for other reasons. "Then I was going to sneak into the house."

Infuriatingly, he grinned. "Tell me, Susan. Why were you going to sneak into your own house?"

"I was going to capture you, of course. I thought you were an intruder."

"And I thought you were an intruder—a clumsy one, at that, what with all the noise you were making. I'm surprised that your neighbors didn't call the police."

"As soon as you let me up, I'll call them myself."

"Susan," he chided, shaking his head. "You wouldn't do that."

"Try me."

"I certainly wouldn't call the police if I found you in my home," Hunter said.

His voice was softer now, much softer, and she felt the warmth of his breath brushing her cheek as he spoke. "What would you do?" she asked, knowing she shouldn't.

Hunter was watching her, his eyes glinting dangerously. "This," he whispered as he lowered his head. His lips lightly brushed hers. "This is the only proper way to deal with an intruder like you."

His mouth closed over hers, fully and firmly this time, reminding her of other times and other places. It was almost as if he was claiming her as his. Again.

Chapter Five

Susan opened her eyes when Hunter stopped kissing her lips and started nibbling at her neck, the way he used to years ago, when she was so crazy in love with him. Or probably she was just crazy, period, back then.

She gradually became aware that Hunter must have released his grasp on her wrists while they were kissing. Her arms were now wound around his waist, while her hands moved with a mind of their own, freely exploring the contours of his back as if memorizing the area for future reference.

Heaven only knew where *his* hands were. They seemed to be everywhere.

"Stop it, Hunter," she said huskily, dropping her hands to her sides and telling them to behave themselves.

"You really want me to stop?" he mumbled.

No, not really. His nibbling was sending wave after wave of delicious shivers through her whole body, and the last thing she wanted was to end the pleasure.

She tried to make her voice more forceful this time. "Yes, Hunter, I really want you to stop."

He stopped. And Susan kept her sigh of regret to herself.

Hunter got to his feet and extended his hand to assist her; after a bare second of indecision, she accepted his offer and gave him her hand. He chuckled as he pulled her up. "Had to think about that for a moment, didn't you?" he said. "Were you afraid I might try to kiss you again?"

"It crossed my mind."

"Mine, too," he admitted with a boyishly endearing grin. He touched her cheek with the back of his fingers, pushing aside her wet hair. "Although, at the moment, you're not the most alluring creature I've ever seen."

"More like a wet hen, I imagine," she agreed. The rain was coming down harder than ever. It felt like icicles hitting her face. "And a cold one, at that."

Hunter held up one hand toward the sky. "I think there's sleet mixed with the rain now."

"I think you're imagining things." She shivered and turned to go inside. She'd taken only a couple of steps when she stumbled, and would have fallen if Hunter hadn't caught her arm in time.

"Are you all right?" he asked anxiously.

"Yes. I must have tripped over something." They both looked down and saw the garden hoe.

"Well, what do you know?" Hunter said. "It *is* a dangerous weapon, after all."

Susan snickered in spite of herself. She started for the house again, with Hunter following closely behind. They made their way up the back steps, across the porch and into the brightly lit kitchen.

"Would you like a cup of coffee?" Hunter asked, raking his long fingers through his thick, dark hair, then shaking his head like a wet puppy. Unlike her, he'd changed from the good clothes he'd worn at lunch. Lucky for him. The chinos and Georgia Tech sweatshirt he now had on were sopping wet, dripping water into his sneakers and onto the tile of her kitchen floor.

Glancing at her, he grinned, and a pang of sheer longing shot through her with a force so strong, she almost couldn't breathe.

"Uh, no thanks, I..." She stopped. "Wait a minute. We're in my house now. You're not supposed to offer *me* coffee."

"Okay. Would you like to offer me a cup?"

"No, I would not."

"It's a little strong, but very good. I made it while I was waiting for you to get home."

She took a deep breath. "What else did you do while you were waiting for me to get home?"

"Oh, I looked around a little. This is a really nice house you have."

"You...!" she said indignantly.

He held up both his hands. "Don't worry. I didn't bother any of your personal stuff."

She wondered what he meant by "didn't bother." Did he mean that he didn't *see* her personal things—especially the intimate items in her bathroom and bedroom—or merely that he didn't *touch* them? She wondered and worried, but didn't dare ask.

Instead, she changed the subject. "Tell me, Hunter. Why did my mother give you a key to my house?"

"She felt sorry for me."

"Beg pardon?"

"After you ran away from our lunch date so abruptly, I didn't have anything else to do, so I stopped by to visit your mother. We had a nice chat."

"Talking about what?" Susan asked.

"You know. This and that."

She narrowed her eyes. "Anything—or anyone—in particular?"

He clicked his tongue. "Mustn't pry, Susan. At any rate, when she found out that I didn't have a place to stay tonight, your mother took pity on me and loaned me her key to your house."

"She...she..." Susan was sputtering, so she stopped and started again. "Why didn't she give you the key to her own house?"

"Susan," he chided. "You know perfectly well that your mother's house is overflowing with guests who came to town for the wedding."

The wedding. *Dear God!* She'd completely forgotten about her own wedding.

She took a deep breath. "Where did you stay last night?"

"A hotel. But I was only able to get the room for one night. They kicked me out today. Did you know that there are three *huge* conventions in town this week?"

"Even if there are, I'm sure—"

Hunter shook his head. "There's not a hotel room to be had within seventy miles of Atlanta. The motel chains are all booked solid, too."

"But surely you know somebody..."

"I used to," Hunter said, shaking his head again. "But it's been two years, you know, and...everything changes. People move away, get married, whatever."

Susan felt a huge lump in her throat. Until that moment, she hadn't comprehended the extent of Hunter's loss—if he was telling the truth and really had had amnesia. She blinked back tears and was glad he was looking at the floor and not at her.

"Your sister!" she exclaimed, suddenly remembering. "Didn't you say Annie still lives here in town?"

He nodded. "Yep. But she and her husband are having their house in Ansley Park completely redone, inside and out. While the work's going on, they're renting a two-bedroom apartment in Buckhead."

"So...?"

"And presently residing in that two-bedroom apartment are my sister, Annie, her husband, Tom, their three boisterous kids and Tom's mother, who's been visiting for the past ten days. When I mentioned my plight to Annie, she immediately replied, 'Don't even think about it.' Does that answer your question?"

"Yes." Susan shook her head. "And I'm sorry. Really I am. But—"

"It's only for one night, Suse," he pleaded.

Suse. She hadn't heard that name in years. Hunter was the only person who'd ever called her that, and he wasn't being fair using it now, knowing how it would bring back old memories.

"You fight dirty," she said.

"I'm a desperate man."

"Okay," she said with a sigh. "You can stay in the guest room tonight."

"Great! I'm sure I'll be able to find another place by tomorrow or the next day—"

"Tomorrow."

"Right. Tomorrow I'll find a place to stay... somehow, someway..."

"Don't overdo it, Hunter. I might change my mind again."

"I'll be on my best behavior. I promise. I'll even let you use the bathroom first."

Susan wasn't surprised that he knew there was only one bathroom in the house. She'd have been surprised if he *hadn't* known. He'd had plenty of time to explore the place at his leisure, without anyone around to interfere. And with his keen architect's eye—coupled with his natural curiosity about everything—he probably knew more about her house than she did.

Glancing down and getting a good look at herself for the first time since they'd come inside, she saw that Hunter wasn't merely being polite. She really *needed* to use the bathroom. Her shoes were caked with mud, her stockings were in shreds and her once-navy dress was barely recognizable, dripping wet and covered with grass stains, red mud, cobwebs and a couple of mystery splotches she'd rather not think about.

"You might want to reconsider," she said. "I'm so filthy, it could take me hours to get clean again."

"I'm in no hurry. It'll give me a chance to move my bags from the front hall to the guest bedroom and get settled in."

"Bags?" she repeated.

"I came by taxi, and had to bring all my stuff with me," Hunter said. "It's kind of nice in a way. I'm fully equipped in case someone invites me to stay awhile."

"Don't hold your breath waiting for that to happen here," Susan replied, stepping out of her mud-caked shoes and dropping them outside on the porch before heading for the bathroom and a long soapy bath.

"SORRY TO TAKE so long," Susan said as she padded into the kitchen.

Hunter looked up from the table where he was sitting drinking coffee and reading a magazine. The sight of her caused him to catch his breath.

There was certainly nothing seductive about the way she was dressed in an oversize terry robe, matching bedroom slippers and a Laura Ashley nightgown peeking out from the top and bottom of the robe. Her cheeks were still pink from her bath, her green eyes were calm and clear and her still-damp chestnut hair was wound loosely atop her head. There was nothing particularly tantalizing about any of that, either. But when you considered the whole package...ah, that was something else.

Freshly scrubbed and void of makeup or artifice, she seemed young, innocent, vulnerable. Well-nigh irresistible.

"It's okay," Hunter croaked, pushing back his chair and getting to his feet. He cleared his throat. "I went ahead and changed into dry clothes, so there was no hurry."

With a sweep of his hand, he indicated his fresh jeans and T-shirt. He was barefoot...and perilously close to baring his emotions, as well. Watching Susan, he saw the change come over her, too, as her gaze swept over him, tip to toe and back again. The way her green eyes darkened told him that she was feeling something. Something.

Take care, Townsend, he cautioned himself.

"Can I get you anything?" he asked.

She shook her head then, as if rousing herself. "I'll get it," she said, her voice husky. She went to the cabinet for a glass, then to the refrigerator to pour herself some milk.

Hunter quickly sat down again and pretended to read the magazine. Out of the corner of his eye, he saw Susan bring her milk to the table and hesitate a moment before taking the seat opposite him. He didn't look up, but could feel her watching him while she drank her milk.

"You've changed," she said when she finished and put the glass on the table.

Hunter raised his head then, and returned her assessing gaze for several seconds before he spoke. "We both have," he finally said. "We're two years older.

Susan had still nearly been a girl when he'd first fallen in love with her. She was tall and slender, with the most marvelous green eyes he'd ever seen, and a wealth of unruly chestnut hair he couldn't resist touching at every opportunity. Back then, she'd been full of contradictions—by turns flirtatious or shy, serious or fun-loving.

Now she was a woman. She was still slender, but the curves he'd seen outlined by her form-fitting wedding gown yesterday, and had felt today while they grappled on the ground in the rain, were the curves of a woman. She had grown up in other ways, too.

He'd remembered her as a schoolgirl, but now she was a competent, successful professional. She was proud of her accomplishments—as she should be—and sure of her ability.

And now she was more experienced, as well. Since Hunter had last seen her, she'd been engaged. Twice. Rambling through her bathroom earlier, he'd accidentally come across the dispenser containing the tiny pills and calendar counter. Shocked at first, then furious, he'd briefly considered throwing the packet away. Luckily, before he could act on his impulse, he'd realized how irrational he was being.

In spite of what he'd told Susan, he knew he had no claim on her. Furthermore, he had no intention of making a claim on her, although he still might see what he could do about sending that stuffed-shirt banker of hers on his way back to Switzerland.

He might not want her for himself, but he wanted her to have someone better than Verner. She deserved more.

"It's more than just being older," Susan said.

It took Hunter a moment to realize she was still talking about how he'd changed. "What, then?"

"There's a determination about you that I never noticed before," she said. "And...and a hardness."

Being handed a death sentence, and later being told that the death sentence was a big lie, will do that to you, Hunter thought. "That's what survival is all about," he said. "Strength—or hardness, as you call it—and determination."

"I suppose," she said, then sighed. "But it's way too late and I'm much too tired to argue about abstracts now."

"I agree," he said, abruptly getting to his feet and heading around the table to stand behind her. "We should stick with the concrete—the basics, such as the fact that you need a neck rub."

"No," she protested.

"You can't fool me, Suse. I've been watching the way you're holding your head, and that little frown between your eyebrows. It's a sure sign you need a neck rub in the worst way."

HUNTER WAS RIGHT, of course, Susan admitted to herself. A neck rub would be heavenly. But not here. Not now. And most especially, not done by him. "It's a bad idea—"

"It's a wonderful idea, and you know it. And if you're worried because your current fiancé is the jealous type and might find out about it, I promise I'll never tell."

"It's not that!" she insisted. And it wasn't. The problem didn't have anything to do with Michael or anyone else. It was hers and hers alone. Bluntly stated, she simply didn't trust herself.

She remembered vividly the way she'd reacted to Hunter's touch earlier. Heaven only knew what she might feel or do if he massaged her now, making her all warm and relaxed, making her respond to his magic fingers...all the while keenly aware of his body-hugging jeans and T-shirt and bare feet. For God's sake, what could be more suggestively intimate than a man in your kitchen in his bare feet!

She shouldn't allow the massage, much as she wanted it. She should tell Hunter that, and put her foot down. She felt his hands on her shoulders, pushing aside her terry robe, and knew it was already too late.

"Unbutton the top of your nightgown and pull it down a little way, Suse," he said softly from right beside her ear. "Just enough so I can get to bare skin."

"I don't see why—"

He snorted. "Nobody can give a proper massage through seven layers of flannel."

Susan did as she was told, giving a little sigh of surrender mixed with anticipation. She closed her eyes.

Hunter's fingers worked their magic the same way they used to—kneading, stroking, manipulating, molding. Susan gave another sigh, this one of pure contentment, and heard Hunter chuckle. She ignored it. She didn't care if he knew he was giving her such sinfully delicious pleasure that she was practically purring. Let him laugh all he wanted to. The massage was worth it.

"Th-th-that's all, folks," Hunter said sometime later.

Susan opened her eyes with a start. "It's over?"

Hunter walked around her chair and leaned his hips against the kitchen table. "Well," he drawled, "I wouldn't necessarily say that." He flexed his fingers and eyed her with speculation. "We've finished with the neck, but if you think other parts of your body need some attention, as well . . . I'm game to continue if you are."

Susan felt the heat rush to her cheeks. She'd been feeling so warm and relaxed, grateful to Hunter, friendly, even . . . and now . . . She pushed back her chair and got up, glaring at him. "Why do you do it?" she asked.

"Do what?"

"Do something nice, like the massage, and then deliberately try to spoil everything by putting it in a sexual context."

Hunter raised his eyebrows. "Was that what I was doing?"

"You know you were."

"And it upset you?"

"Yes."

"Good."

"What?" she asked in disbelief.

"That means you still care."

Susan opened her mouth to speak, but her mind chose that moment to go completely blank. She closed her mouth and stalked out of the kitchen and down the hall, instead.

"Are you going to bed now?" Hunter called after her.

She silently continued to her bedroom. "G'night!" she heard him call just before she slammed the door behind her.

Closing her eyes, Susan leaned her back against the door. She stood perfectly still, listening to the sound of her heart pounding against her chest, listening to the lingering echo of his voice taunting, "That means you still care."

Damn Hunter Townsend!

And damn him especially for guessing the truth— she *did* still care for him. Heaven help her.

Chapter Six

Susan took several deep breaths, willing herself to calm down. There was no way that Hunter could actually know for sure that she cared for him. He'd made a wild accusation, probably just to needle her, and had accidentally touched a nerve. That was all.

And that was what it would remain.

He'd waltzed back into her life suddenly, catching her by surprise. Off guard, she'd been susceptible to him, but now that she was aware of the situation, she could handle it.

After all, she'd survived the loss of him once before, at a time when her entire world revolved around him. If she could survive that, she could survive anything. Besides, she was older now, stronger, and perhaps even wiser.

Getting over him this time might not be a cinch, but it could be done. And she would do it.

With that comforting thought, Susan padded over to her bed. She took off her robe and slippers and climbed between the cool, clean sheets. She'd just reached up and turned off the bedside lamp, when another thought struck her like a bolt of lightning.

Even if she could get over Hunter, as she'd confidently convinced herself she could, what did the fact that she cared for him now—cared anything at all—say about her relationship with Michael?

She admired and respected Michael, and had come to love him. True, theirs wasn't a grand passion such as she'd known with Hunter. But a bright, shining, all-consuming love like that could only come once in a lifetime, and once it burned itself out, you were never quite the same.

That's why Susan had felt herself lucky to find Michael, who was kind, caring and compatible. She had thought what they shared together was enough, but now she wondered. If she truly loved him the way a woman is supposed to love the man she's going to share the rest of her life with, would she still feel this attraction to Hunter? Or to any other man?

Not likely.

Was that what her mother had been trying to tell her yesterday before the ceremony?

A sudden knocking at her bedroom door roused Susan from her thoughts. It had to be Hunter.

"Susan?"

It was.

"Are you asleep?" he called.

"I'm trying to be."

"I just thought I'd let you know it's not raining anymore."

"You disturbed me to tell me *that?*" she groused.

"It's snowing instead."

"Snowing?" she repeated. "It's too late in the year to snow here."

"I know. Still, it's coming down like crazy. Wanna go outside and build a snowman?"

She smiled in the dark. "I'd rather wait till morning."

"All the snow might be gone by then."

"I'll take my chances. Go to bed, Hunter."

"I meant to tell you," he said. "The mattress in the guest room is way too soft."

"Try the sofa then."

"I did. It's too short."

"Too bad," she said, totally unsympathetic.

"I tried your bed earlier this afternoon," he said hopefully. "It's perfect."

"It's also occupied."

"It's a big bed . . ."

"Not big enough. Now go away and let me sleep."

"You're not being very hospitable."

"So sue me. But *go!*"

"I'm going, I'm going," he grumbled.

Susan heard him shuffle away, still grumbling. Some things about Hunter hadn't changed. He still loved to argue. She smiled again. At least the interruption had taken her mind off her problem with Michael. She decided to worry about it tomorrow when she was rested and her mind was clear.

She punched up her pillow and rolled onto her side, heaving a huge sigh as she closed her eyes.

Then it hit her.

She opened her eyes and bolted upright in bed.

She couldn't postpone worrying about her problem with Michael until tomorrow.

He was coming to her house for breakfast tomorrow!

Not only that, but Hunter undoubtedly would still be here, too.

"Oh, hell."

She could picture the two of them—the three of them if you counted her—in one big knock-down-and-drag-out brouhaha. But maybe she'd get lucky. Maybe she'd suddenly vanish into the woodwork. Or maybe she'd be whisked away in a spaceship before Michael arrived.

HUNTER SLEPT only fitfully and was wide-awake by dawn. It wasn't the soft mattress that bothered him most; it was the owner of the soft mattress. He kept having erotic dreams about her, disturbing what little sleep he got.

The more he thought about it, the more convinced he became that conniving his way into her house had been a lousy idea, although it had seemed inspired when he first thought of it. He had planned to use their time alone together to reestablish a relationship with her, regain her confidence and then enlist her help in exposing her stepfather.

He was using her, granted, but he'd had no qualms about that. Why should he? Two years ago, she'd promised to love him forever. But with her, forever had lasted only a few months. Then, quick as a wink, she was engaged to someone else. And now she was engaged to yet another man.

With the kind of track record she had, why should he feel any loyalty to her? And if he happened to hurt her, why should he feel compassion? He shouldn't.

Yet even as he told himself all that, Hunter knew he didn't believe a damned word of it. In spite of everything, he still cared for her. And if he stayed around long enough, he had the sinking feeling he'd come to care a lot more. The best thing for him to do was get the hell out of her house as quickly as he could, like right now before she woke up.

Hunter decided that was exactly what he would do. Stretching and yawning, he threw back the blanket and got out of bed. He reached down to gather the jeans he'd left on the floor. Pulling them on, he yawned again, scratched his bare stomach and ambled over to the window to lift the blinds.

He looked out the window, rubbed his eyes, then looked again, unable to believe what he was seeing.

"Damn!" he finally muttered. "It's a real blizzard!"

He'd told Susan last night that it was snowing outside. But the weather had been so warm earlier that he'd never expected the snow to stick, or to continue coming down for long. He'd been wrong on both counts.

It was hard to believe. Who'd ever heard of such snow as this in Georgia in the middle of March? The ground was covered, the trees, everything in sight. He couldn't even tell where Susan's yard ended and the street began. And it was still coming down so hard that visibility was practically zero.

"Holy cow," he muttered, shaking his head.

Hunter remembered how snowstorms, even small ones, used to bring Atlanta traffic to a halt because the city had no equipment to keep the streets open. One car would stall or spin out, then another, and soon an entire thoroughfare would be blocked. He doubted if the situation had changed very much in the two years he'd been away. Which meant, if he was going to leave at all, he'd have to do it before the streets became snarled with traffic accidents. He needed to call a taxi immediately.

He would dress and write Susan a goodbye note
while he was waiting for the taxi to arrive. He started
for the door, planning to use the telephone in the hall,
but stopped after only a few steps.

He couldn't do it. He couldn't leave her alone right
in the middle of a raging storm. And he certainly
couldn't leave her with only a brief note of explanation. It was true that he'd left her once before with *no*
explanation, but that was completely different.

With a sigh of resignation, Hunter turned around
and retraced his steps. He gathered his shaving kit and
headed for the bathroom. He was too wide-awake to
go back to sleep now, so he might as well take his
shower before Susan got up. Then he'd go to the
kitchen and see what he could rustle up for breakfast.

"WHAT ON EARTH are you doing?" Susan asked
breathlessly. After a sleepless night, she'd finally
dozed around dawn, only to be awakened by clamor-
ing sounds a short while later. Barely pausing to throw
on her robe, she'd raced to the kitchen to see what was
happening.

Hunter was on his hands and knees with his head
and upper torso poked inside one of her bottom
kitchen cabinets, so she was forced to address her
question to his backside. In spite of a wicked headache caused by lack of sleep, she couldn't help noticing what an attractive backside it was, all muscle and
no fat, filling out his faded jeans to perfection.

At the sound of her voice, Hunter jumped, hitting
his head on something. He muttered an expletive and
backed out of the cabinet. "What does it look like I'm
doing?"

"Beats me," she replied, raising both hands.

"I'm trying to find a suitable pot to cook the damned oatmeal in," he said, as if explaining it to a ten-year-old.

"Oatmeal?"

"That's all I could find for breakfast. Did you know your refrigerator is almost completely empty? No bacon, no eggs or butter. You're even out of milk, for heaven's sake!"

"I know," she replied with exaggerated sweetness. "I tried to throw away everything that was perishable."

"You—"

"If you recall, I hadn't planned to be here," she continued. "I'd planned to be far away by now. On my honeymoon."

Hunter got to his feet, bringing a stainless-steel pot up with him. "You could at least have left a few necessities."

"I thought I did. You found oatmeal, didn't you?"

"Sure." He measured water into the pot, placed it on a burner, then turned on the stove. "And it's going to taste just dandy with no milk."

She shrugged and padded across the kitchen to the counter, hoping he wouldn't notice she was barefoot. "I see you made coffee." She poured herself a cup. "This is really all I want."

"For how long?"

"What?"

"How long are you going to be happy on a steady diet of coffee and nothing else?"

"After I finish my coffee, I'll get dressed and go to the market," she said. "On the way, I can drop you off wherever you want to go. Okay?"

Hunter dumped oatmeal into the pot and stirred it before replying. "Not okay."

"What do you mean?"

"It's still snowing."

"I can see that," she said impatiently. "But I'm sure the snow will melt later this morning when the temperature goes up."

"I wouldn't count on it," Hunter replied, taking her by the elbow. "Come with me."

Susan was too surprised to protest. "Where are we going?"

"Just to the front of the house. Your porch hides the view in back."

"My feet are cold."

"It'll only take a minute."

Hunter led her to the living room and the large double windows covered by full-length drapes. He paused a moment for effect, then pulled a cord to open the drapes.

Susan gasped.

"See what I mean?" Hunter said, pointing to the snowstorm raging outside her windows.

"You don't have to point. I can see that it's snowing."

"More than that," he said, sounding pleased. "This almost reminds me of the Antarctic."

"It won't last long."

"That's what I thought, too, last night. Now I'm not so sure. From the looks of things, it could go on for hours."

"The snow will start melting by 10:00 a.m.," she predicted.

"The temperature has dropped a degree in the last hour," he said, moving away from the window and turning his attention to her.

Susan combed her fingers through her hair, suddenly aware of how she must look. She pulled her robe together tighter around her. "How do you know that?" she asked sharply. She didn't know why she blamed Hunter, holding him responsible for the ghastly weather. She just did.

"Well, I'm not certain. I was going by the thermometer outside your kitchen window, but it could be wrong. You should know."

He'd neatly turned the tables on her with that remark. She couldn't think of a cutting response, so she retreated. "I'm going to get dressed."

"Don't forget your coffee," Hunter called after her. "And the oatmeal will probably be ready by the time you are."

Susan considered escaping directly to her bedroom, but then thought better of it. A good hot cup of coffee was more important than pride. She went back to the kitchen for her coffee, before heading to her bedroom.

Susan took her time getting dressed, not because she wanted to look especially good for Hunter's benefit, but because she dreaded facing him again. Nobody had a right to look as good as he did this early in the morning. She was sure he'd thrown on the first clothes he found, too—the same jeans he'd changed into last night, loafers without socks and a maroon crewneck sweater she was almost sure she recognized from two years ago.

On him, it all looked marvelous. By comparison, she'd felt like Old Mother Hubbard in her nightgown and robe. So maybe she *did* want him to see her in a better light. So what?

On the other hand, she didn't want him to *know* she'd chosen a particular outfit for his benefit.

The hell with it! she finally decided, pulling on a pair of gray flannel slacks and an oxford button-down shirt. She was trying to decide whether a cardigan tied loosely around her shoulders would be too much, when she heard the phone ring.

It was probably Michael, calling about their breakfast plans! She raced to the bedroom door and threw it open. "Don't answer the phone!" she called to Hunter. "I'll get—"

She was too late. The phone had already stopped ringing and she could hear the low rumble of Hunter's voice in the kitchen. A few moments later, he ambled into the hall, holding the portable phone she kept on the kitchen counter.

"It's for you. I think it's your fiancé," he added in a loud stage whisper.

She snatched the instrument from his hands and retreated into her bedroom, slamming the door behind her. She closed her eyes and took a deep breath before speaking. "Michael?"

"Was that Townsend on the phone?" Michael said without preamble.

"Uh, yes."

"He said it was, but I didn't believe him. What's *he* doing there?"

He sounded very angry. Furious, in fact. "Well," she began, trying to decide where to start to explain.

"He said he spent the night there, but I didn't believe that, either."

She was starting to get angry, herself. "He was telling the truth."

"*Susan!* How could you?"

How could you? She wondered how he'd come up with that old chestnut. Did Michael think in those terms when he was angry? "How could I what?"

"How could you allow yourself to be exposed to that...that charlatan!"

That did it. "*Exposed?*" she repeated, pouncing on the word. "It's not as if he's contagious."

"You know what I mean."

"No, I don't know what you mean. What is it, exactly, that you think I did, Michael?"

"You let that stranger come into your house—"

"Hunter is *not* a stranger. I've known him a lot longer than I've known you. And yes, I did let him come into my house."

"He spent the night there, for God's sake! What will people say?"

Susan wasn't sure she trusted herself to speak. "Listen to me, Michael, and listen well. Hunter Townsend, a man I've known for years, a man I used to love, spent the night in my guest bedroom last night. I invited him because he had no place else to stay. He slept in his room and I slept in my room. *And I don't give a flying damn what people say!*"

She pushed the Off switch on the phone as hard as she could, wishing it was a regular phone so she could slam down the receiver. She counted to ten, opened the bedroom door and stalked across the hall to the kitchen.

Hunter was standing by the kitchen sink looking out the window, but turned around as soon as she came into the room. He smiled, and opened his mouth to say something.

"You!" she said before he had a chance to speak. She pointed her finger directly at him and glared. "Don't say a word! I warn you. *Not one word!"*

He nodded.

Susan stalked over to the counter and replaced the portable phone in its cradle, then turned to Hunter.

"And remember this. This is my house. My telephone. And I'm the only person who answers my telephone in my house! Understand?"

Hunter gave her a smart salute. "Aye, aye, sir."

Chapter Seven

"Are you sure you won't have some oatmeal?" Hunter asked, wiping his mouth with a napkin.

Susan, who was sitting across the kitchen table from him, shook her head and took another sip of coffee. Oatmeal had never been high on her list of favorite foods, and at the moment she was much too upset to eat anything at all. She wished she hadn't hung up on Michael, although his attitude had merited such treatment. It was just that she considered hanging up on someone the height of rudeness, and almost never did it.

"No, thanks," she said.

"I found a can of sweetened condensed milk in your cabinet, and dumped that in, along with a few spices. It's surprisingly good," he added with a grin.

"I'm sure it is," she agreed, wondering if she should call Michael back. After all, she *had* invited him to breakfast. She needed to know whether he still planned to come.

"It's almost like eating dessert," Hunter said, still talking about his concoction. "Maybe I should call it Oatmeal Surprise and sell the recipe."

Susan laughed. "Tell me, Hunter. Who would buy a recipe for oatmeal?"

"Lots of people," he said, looking offended. "Famous chefs and restaurants...or maybe I'll simply skip the middleman and publish a collection of recipes myself."

She nodded. "That sounds like the ticket."

"I'll hire your agency to handle promotion for my book."

"Wow."

"Tell me," he said, turning his head to one side, then the other. "Which side do you think will look better on the book jacket?"

"Neither. I'd go full-face if I were you. It looks more sincere, and you know how important sincerity is in cooking."

"Right," Hunter agreed, resting his chin in his hand and leaning across the table to gaze into her eyes, sincerely. "How's this?" he asked.

"Be *more* sincere," she suggested with a giggle.

"Like this?" He tilted his chin to one side, poked out his lower lip and screwed up his eyebrows in such a way that he seemed to be in pain.

"Perfect!" Susan announced when she was able to stop laughing.

Hunter nodded and got up. "Ready for your Oatmeal Surprise now?"

"I'll have some later," Susan promised. She got up, too. "But first, I need to make a phone call. I'll use the phone in the hall."

She was still smiling as she marched down the hall to telephone Michael. He answered on the first ring. She wondered if he'd been sitting by the phone, waiting for her to call and apologize. "It's Susan," she said quickly. "I'm sorry I hung up on you."

She heard his sharp intake of breath, and could almost picture him bristling, but he said nothing. "Michael, are you still there?"

"Hanging up the way you did was rude."

His voice was so pompous that Susan found it hard to be contrite. "Yes."

"Terribly rude."

"I've already said I was sorry."

"Very well. We'll put it behind us."

She fell silent, waiting for him to apologize, too, for his suspicions about what happened between Hunter and her last night and all his concern about what the neighbors might think. Personally, she thought he had more to apologize for than she did.

But then she remembered the kiss she and Hunter had exchanged, the neck rub he'd given her and the emotions those things had aroused deep inside her. "That's all I called to say. I think I'll go have breakfast now."

"You invited me to come to your house for breakfast."

"That's right," she said. She'd completely forgotten. "Are you coming?"

"In this weather? Haven't you looked outside?"

What did he think? That she'd been in bed with Hunter all morning and didn't know there was a snowstorm? "Of course I've looked outside. But I assumed—with your being from Switzerland—that you'd be able to drive in a little snow."

"It's not my ability to drive that's in question here," Michael said.

"It's not?"

"It's all your other crazy Atlanta drivers. They speed like maniacs, and have no idea how to handle their vehicles. They slip and slide all over the place in weather like this."

"I see. And you're afraid one of them might slide right into your Mercedes and dent your fender."

"It's more than that—"

"Dent your door?"

"Susan," he warned.

"Just kidding," she said, relenting. "I see your point. And you shouldn't try to drive in this weather."

"Perhaps the snow will melt later in the day."

"I'm sure it will."

"I'll come over then," Michael said.

"Fine. I'll look forward to seeing you."

"We can make a final decision on a new date for our wedding."

"Well," she said, hedging, "I'm not sure about that. There are so many things to consider."

"Is Townsend still there?" Michael asked abruptly.

"Yes. But what does that have to do with anything?"

"The two of you are there in the house alone?" he asked accusingly.

"No. The king and queen dropped by for tea," she said. "Of course we're alone, Michael. What are you getting at?"

"I would have thought he'd be gone by now."

"I don't know why you'd think that. You said yourself that the weather's too bad to drive in right now," Susan said, permitting herself a smile of satisfaction.

"Yes...well, uh, I imagine the weather will improve soon."

"I imagine," she agreed.

"I'll be over there as soon as it does," he said.

"Okay. But be sure to call before you come."

"What?"

"I might be outside building a snowman. Bye." Without waiting for his reply, Susan gently replaced the hall phone in its cradle.

She shook her head, wondering whether it was something new, or if Michael had always been pompous and stuffy and she just hadn't noticed it until now. She sighed, then smiled as she headed back to the kitchen for a big bowl of Oatmeal Surprise.

Hunter was on his hands and knees peering inside her cabinet once more.

"You really have a thing for my kitchen cabinet, don't you?" she commented.

At the sound of her voice, he jumped, hitting his head on something again. He backed out of the cabinet and looked up at her with a scowl. "You really enjoy causing me to do bodily harm to myself, don't you?"

"I'm sorry," she said, walking over to stand beside him. "Are you all right?"

He rubbed the back of his head where he'd hit it for the second time. "No permanent damage, I guess."

"Were you looking for something in particular?"

"Yeah." He held out his hand and she pulled him to his feet. "Do you have something big enough for soup?"

He was still holding her hand. She gently tugged it loose. "I have a soup pot," she said. "Will that do?"

Hunter snapped his fingers. "Eureka!"

Susan walked over to another cabinet and pulled out a big covered pot. "Would it be rude for me to ask what you intend doing with this?'' She handed him the pot.

''I'm going to make soup, of course.''

''Two questions,'' she said. ''Why? And what are you going to use for ingredients?''

''Number one, there's a good possibility we'll be stranded here for some time.''

''I don't think—''

''Don't think, Susan. Just listen to me. The temperature's falling and so is the snow. Like crazy. And your power could go off at any time. The lights have already flickered a couple of times while you were on the telephone.''

The lights chose that particular instant to flicker again.

''See what I mean?'' Hunter said.

Susan nodded as the seriousness of the situation started to dawn on her.

''As for ingredients...'' Hunter stepped over to the counter and picked up an onion she hadn't noticed before. ''I found this treasure in the vegetable bin of your refrigerator.''

''One onion?''

''There's an old saying that sailors use when they're on a long voyage. 'To make anything, you start with an onion.' I found a couple of carrots, too. You must have decided they wouldn't spoil while you were away.''

She nodded. ''But that's not enough to make soup.''

''No, but it's enough to *season* soup. And I found some dried peas in your pantry.''

Susan nodded again. ''I planned to cook them last New Year's for good luck, but never got around to it.''

"It's a good thing you didn't. They've brought you good luck now." Hunter carried the pot over to the sink, filled it with water, then put it on the stove. "The peas need to cook a long time, so we'll put them on first. They can be cooking while you eat your oatmeal."

"You were so excited about the soup, I thought you'd forgotten my Oatmeal Surprise."

"Not me," he said, serving her oatmeal and directing her to sit. "I never forget important things."

Susan looked at Hunter. He looked at her. She knew they were thinking about the same thing. She saw pain in his dark eyes.

"The amnesia . . ." Hunter stopped and cleared his throat. "That was different."

"I know," she said softly, reaching out to touch his arm. "It wasn't your fault."

Hunter hesitated, looking as if he was going to say something else. But he didn't. Instead, he nodded his head, then turned and walked over to the sink. Susan watched his back for long moments. Then she blinked, took a deep breath and started eating her oatmeal.

When she was in control of herself again, she looked in Hunter's direction. He was watching her. "You were right," she said. "This is really good. Delicious. You'll make a fortune on your cookbook."

"And you'll handle the promotion."

"You bet. We'll both make a fortune."

Hunter grinned. "Right." He poured the peas into the boiling water. "In the meantime, as soon as you finish eating, you might see what else you can find to add to the soup."

Susan frowned. "Probably not much. I usually buy fresh things that I can eat right away."

"We could really, really use a can of tomatoes, if you have one."

As soon as she finished her oatmeal, Susan washed her bowl and started searching the cupboards in the pantry. There were no canned tomatoes, but she did find tomato juice and two jars of California organic sun-dried tomatoes.

"I don't see why they wouldn't work," Hunter said. "They'll probably puff up like tomatoes fresh from the garden."

Susan laughed. "Where did you learn to cook, Hunter?"

"Aboard a sailing ship," he said, stirring the peas and adding salt and pepper. "At sea, you throw in everything you can find." He stirred the peas again, then added another dash of salt.

"And?" she prompted.

"Somehow or other, it turns out to be delicious."

"But we're not at sea," she said.

"We might as well be," he said, pointing to the window, where the snow could be seen coming down stronger than ever.

Marooned. The word flashed into Susan's mind from nowhere. Once planted, it wouldn't budge. She and Hunter were marooned. In this house. Alone. *For how long?*

"I'll see what else I can find for the soup," she said, scurrying back to the relative safety of the pantry.

Susan had located only a few more items when the phone rang again. Hunter, undoubtedly recalling her earlier outburst, made no move to answer it. "I'll get it," she said unnecessarily as she headed to the hall and picked up the receiver.

"Hello, Susan."

"Kenneth!" she exclaimed, recognizing her step-father's voice. "What a nice surprise."

"I was worried about you, what with this terrible storm we're having. Are you all right?"

"I'm fine. Are *you?*"

"Oh, yes. It's a bit lonesome rattling around in this big old house with only the servants for company, but otherwise I'm doing well."

When Kenneth had married her mother, the two of them had decided to live in the Willingham home on Habersham Road rather than his family estate on West Paces Ferry Road. Luckily, Kenneth had chosen to rent out the Brantley home rather than sell it, so he was able to move back there after the divorce.

"I'm glad you're not alone," Susan said. In spite of the divorce, she and her stepfather had remained on friendly terms.

"I understand you're not alone, either," he said.

Susan frowned, wondering why Michael had told her stepfather about Hunter spending the night at her house. It had to have been Michael who told. Even though Susan's mother had loaned Hunter a key to the house, she had no way of knowing whether or not he'd spent the night.

"You talked to Michael?" she asked.

"He's concerned about you, Susan, and so am I."

"There's nothing to be concerned about."

"Frankly," he continued, ignoring her protest, "I find it hard to believe that you would allow Town-send to come anywhere near you, much less permit him to spend the night in your home."

Susan's cheeks flamed. "Surely Michael must have told you that nothing happened between us."

"That's beside the point. The two of you were there—alone. You can imagine how that would look to everybody."

"Including you?"

"Certainly not. You know I've always been on your side, Susan. Don't you?"

"Yes," she whispered. That's what she'd always thought before. Now, for the first time, she wondered.

"I've tried to be a father to you. And, like a father, I won't permit anyone to hurt you."

"Hunter wouldn't—"

"Did you hear me? *I won't allow it!*"

Shocked by Kenneth Brantley's uncustomary outburst, it took Susan a moment to recover. "Hunter is no danger to me," she stated.

"How can you say that? After what he did to you!"

"Maybe he didn't—"

"Of course he did! He deserted you, left you standing at the altar like some poor, pitiful creature. He made you a laughingstock, Susan! Have you forgotten that?"

"No. But he said—"

"*He* said! The man's a liar, Susan! He's a cheat and a charlatan. You can't believe a word he says."

"What if he really did have amnesia?" she asked, feeling as if she were drowning, fighting for her life.

"*Rubbish!* You know better than that. It's another of his lies."

"I thought it was at first, but now..."

"Nothing's changed. Whatever Townsend is saying now is only his desperate attempt to confuse you. Don't believe it."

Susan was breathing hard, and could hear her step-father's labored breathing over the phone. She'd never heard him talk like this before. It was a side to Kenneth Brantley she'd never known. "I...I'll think about it," she said.

"You do that," Kenneth said, more in control of himself now. "Use your own good sense."

"Yes."

"And for goodness' sake, *get Hunter Townsend out of that house as fast as you can!*"

"Goodbye, Kenneth," she said, not promising anything. Her hand trembled as she replaced the telephone in its cradle.

She tried to think, but she was too upset to make much sense of anything at the moment. Only one thing was abundantly clear—Kenneth didn't merely dislike Hunter. He hated him. Much more than she'd ever imagined.

HUNTER STOOD at the kitchen counter with his gaze trained on the small screen of the portable TV. So far, he'd found television sets in every room of Susan's house except the dining room and bathroom. Maybe she had them stashed in those rooms, too, cleverly disguised as silver chests or clothes hampers or such.

He presumed that Susan's job necessitated such a conspicuous display of the electronic medium, but he couldn't help grinning when he remembered her elit-ist disdain for the "boob tube" while she was in col-lege. How times change, he thought. And how people change.

He leaned closer to the set as soon as the commer-cial ended and the news announcer reappeared. "Storm of the century, sweeping across much of the

South, leaving thousands without power... Winter storm warning for the entire metro area as snow continues to fall."

Hearing a noise behind him, Hunter turned to see Susan coming into the kitchen. She was almost as white as the snow falling outside the window. He switched off the TV and hurried toward her. She swayed just as he reached her. He didn't know whether she would have fallen if he hadn't been there, but he pulled her against him and held on tight.

"I'm all right," she said, her voice low and throaty.

"No, you're not." He felt a tremor go through her and tightened his arm around her shoulders. He reached up his other hand to touch her hair, then gently guided her head to his chest. "Relax," he murmured. "Just take a deep breath and then let it out slowly."

She did as he told her. "Good," he said, stroking her hair. He could feel her starting to relax in his arms.

"Now take another deep breath," Hunter ordered. He took one with her this time, and inhaled the sweet fresh scent of her hair. He closed his eyes, savoring the moment as the familiar fragrance brought back a flood of bittersweet memories.

He smiled.

Then he frowned, wondering whose phone call it was that had caused her such distress. It could have been Michael Verner calling again, but somehow he didn't think so. She'd already talked to him a couple of times. She'd been angry after the first time, and pretty satisfied with herself after the second, which had taken place only shortly before the last phone call.

Neither of her chats with her current fiancé had disturbed her the way the last phone call had. He also dismissed the idea that a call from Susan's mother would have upset her so much. Even though the two of them might disagree on occasion, they had a solid mother-daughter relationship based on mutual love, trust and understanding.

The caller had to have been someone close to Susan; otherwise, the conversation wouldn't have upset her so much. If it wasn't Verner, and it wasn't Mrs. Brantley...then who was it? Her stepfather?

Hunter considered that possibility. In spite of the divorce, Susan had remained close to Kenneth Brantley. And she'd attacked Hunter like a tigress when he'd mentioned her stepfather in connection with Dr. Estep and his headaches. So Brantley had the *power* to upset Susan. But why would he want to? Did he somehow know that Hunter had spent the night with her?

That information could have come through Verner...*if* Susan's fiancé and stepfather were on familiar terms. Knowing how Brantley felt about him, Hunter was sure the man would have chastised Susan severely for allowing him in her house, much less permitting him to spend the night.

Lost in thought, Hunter was startled when the telephone rang again. Susan almost jumped out of her skin. She raised her head and looked at him with dark, troubled eyes. Neither of them spoke. The phone rang again. And again.

"Will you answer it?" Susan finally asked. "Please?"

Hunter nodded, but guided her to a seat at the kitchen table before moving over to pick up the portable phone. "Hello," he said cautiously.

"Hunter?"

"Yes."

"This is Helen Brantley. It seems that the key I loaned you did the trick."

"Beg pardon?" he asked.

"Since you're at Susan's house this morning, and I hear that the roads are almost impassable, I assume you spent the night there."

He glanced in Susan's direction. She was watching him. "It's your mother," he said silently, mouthing the words. Susan nodded and picked up the magazine he'd been reading earlier. Even if she wasn't paying attention to his conversation, he knew she could hear every word he spoke.

"That's correct," he said into the phone.

"Well, you told me you were desperate for some time alone with my daughter. You had some important questions you wanted to ask her. That's why I loaned you my key. Remember?"

"Of course."

"So—were you able to find out from her what you wanted to know?"

"Not exactly."

"Why are you being so... *Oh!* Is Susan in the same room? Can she hear what you're saying?"

"Oh, yes."

"I see. And you don't want to reveal anything that would make her think that you and I are coconspirators, so to speak?"

"Absolutely."

She sighed. "Well... is there *anything* you can tell me?"

"I woke up early this morning and the snow was coming down so hard I could barely see the street from the window of the guest room. I'm not sure what time

Susan got up, but I'd already made coffee by the time she came across the hall to the kitchen from her bedroom."

Mrs. Brantley laughed. "Neatly phrased, Hunter. That takes care of the sleeping arrangements. What else?"

"I made oatmeal for breakfast. Then the lights started flickering and I was afraid the power would go out, so we started making some soup. We've almost finished putting it together."

"It all sounds deadly dull to me."

"Well . . . you asked." Out of the corner of his eye, Hunter saw Susan get up and leave the kitchen. "I'm alone for the moment," he said, lowering his voice. "What was it you wanted to know?"

"What are your intentions?"

He blinked with surprise. "Concerning Susan?"

"Of course concerning Susan. Why did you feel it was so urgent that you spend time alone with her?"

Hunter took a deep breath. "Truthfully, I'd hoped to reestablish a relationship with her . . . I mean, only in the sense that we'd be friends again," he added quickly.

"And that's all?"

"No. Then I'd hoped to enlist her support. I wanted her to help me."

"And you thought she would?"

"Why not?"

"Well, you did walk out on her two years ago."

"But I had amnesia then. I—"

"Hunter," she interrupted. "You needn't try to keep up that charade with me."

"Charade? You were the one who said I had amnesia in the first place."

"I only suggested it, and only as a favor to you to help you out of a tight spot. It doesn't mean I believed it. I know full well that you never had amnesia. At least, you didn't have it when you tried to contact Susan from someplace in South America."

"You knew about that? But how? Did your husband...?"

"I was out of town at the time you called," Mrs. Brantley said. "The maid told me as soon as I returned the following week. I tried to contact you immediately, but you'd already left by then, and nobody seemed to know where you could be reached."

"I couldn't be reached," Hunter said. "I'd already signed on aboard a schooner bound for Australia."

"Hunter, there's something you should know. I didn't tell Susan that you'd tried to get in touch with her."

"I understand," he said. "After all, she was engaged to someone else at the time."

"No. That wasn't it. The truth is, I didn't tell her because I didn't know for sure *why* you had called...whether it was to try and patch things up between the two of you or not. I decided that if you did want to get back together, you'd call again. And if you didn't...she'd be better off not even knowing you'd called."

There was a long pause. Hunter tried to think of something to say, but came up blank.

"So I didn't tell her," Mrs. Brantley continued. "I couldn't bear seeing her the way she was the first time you left. She was devastated."

Devastated? Hunter tried to grapple with the idea of that. It was something that had never occurred to him.

"You do understand, don't you?" Susan's mother asked.

"Yes," he lied. "Yes, of course I do."

"Good. I'm glad we cleared the air. So tell me, what is it you want Susan to help you with now?"

Hunter shook his head, trying to make sense of the jumbled thoughts flying around inside it. "I'm not sure," he said. He cleared his throat. "Something happened two years ago. It may have been an honest mistake…or it could have been deliberate. I intend to find out."

"I'm afraid you've lost me."

"I'm sorry, but it's complicated and I think it's best…for you…that I don't tell you any more at this stage. I'd just be guessing, anyway."

"But you will tell me when—and if—you find out?"

"It's a promise," he vowed.

"And in the meantime, will you promise me something else, Hunter?"

"If I can."

"Don't hurt Susan again."

Hunter swallowed. "I'll…I'll try my best not to."

"You do that. And remember—hell hath no fury like the mother of a woman scorned *for the second time!*"

"I—"

"Bye now."

Hunter heard the click when she hung up, but didn't move for a long time. He simply stared at the phone he held in his hand.

Susan walked back into the kitchen…convenient timing if he'd ever seen it. He was sure she hadn't eavesdropped. That would have been totally out of character, but she might have heard something as she'd approached the kitchen. He thought about the conversation and decided Susan couldn't have heard anything important because her mother had been doing most of the talking then. He replaced the portable phone in its cradle.

"Was Mother all right?" Susan asked.

"Yes. She was just checking to see if things were okay here. I told her we were making soup, and everything was—"

Hunter never finished the sentence—and Susan wouldn't have heard him, anyway—because just then there was an earsplitting, window-rattling crash outside. Susan screamed just as the lights went out.

Chapter Eight

"Stay here!" Hunter commanded. With that, he ran out of the kitchen and down the hall.

Pausing only long enough to catch her breath, Susan tore out after him. By the time she was halfway down the hall, he was already opening the front door.

"Wait for me!" she yelled. He didn't, but did leave the door open for her to follow. She ran through the doorway and onto the front porch, where she stopped dead in her tracks.

"Good grief!" she said.

Hunter, poised at the bottom of the steps, turned and came back up to stand beside her. They stared at the huge fallen tree lying across her driveway and covering much of her front yard. The tree's roots, along with an enormous gaping hole, were visible in her next-door neighbor's yard.

Neither Susan nor Hunter spoke for a long time. She was too stunned to speak, and supposed he was, too. "It looks like an oak tree," he finally commented.

Susan nodded. "Yes. It was almost a hundred years old."

He whistled. "A terrible pity."

"I need to take a closer look and see what damage has been done," Susan said, making a move toward the steps.

Hunter reached out his arm to stop her. "You need to go back in the house and get properly dressed before you do anything."

In the excitement, Susan had forgotten she wasn't dressed for snow and freezing temperatures. "You're right," she said, shivering as she headed inside the house to put on some warm clothes. Hunter followed her.

"I see the lights have come back on," he observed as they entered the house and he closed the door behind them.

"Thank goodness," she said.

"I wouldn't count on them staying on, though."

"Don't be such a pessimist," Susan said, heading for her bedroom while Hunter stopped at the guest room. She'd taken only a few steps, when the lights flickered and then went off again. She turned around to look at Hunter, who was standing in the doorway to the guest room.

He shrugged. "What can I say?"

Shaking her head, Susan continued walking to her bedroom, where she searched out the warmest garments she could find. She'd already put away most of her winter clothes, but was able to find an all-weather jacket with a hood, along with a long cashmere scarf and her hiking boots.

When she left the house a little later, Hunter was waiting on the steps, and she saw several neighbors gathered in the street to observe the fallen tree. She waved to them and started down the steps.

Hunter held out his hand. "Watch—"

Just then, Susan's feet slipped out from under her. She frantically grabbed for Hunter's outstretched hand but missed, landing painfully on her rear end and sliding down the rest of the steps.

By the time Susan reached the ground, Hunter was already kneeling beside her. "I was going to tell you that the steps were slippery," he said.

"Thanks for the warning."

"Are you all right?"

"I think so," she said, lifting one hip to rub her rear end. "Although my, uh, pride may be a little bruised."

Hunter helped her to her feet, and held on to her arm while she took a few tentative steps. "I'm okay. Really," she assured him. "Let's take a closer look at the tree."

They started across her front lawn, which had been sprouting new green growth yesterday but was now covered with several inches of snow. Hunter still kept his grip on her arm, and she didn't object. The going was slippery and she had no desire to fall again.

"I wonder why your next-door neighbors haven't come outside. The tree must belong to them—or it did—and surely they heard the noise."

"They're away on vacation," Susan replied. "Their kids have spring break this week and they all went to the Caribbean."

"Lucky neighbors. Which reminds me—where did you say you and Verner were planning to spend your honeymoon?"

She gave him a sharp look. "If you don't remember, it's none of your business."

"For our honeymoon—yours and mine," he said, "I've been dreaming about a beautiful little island I once visited in the South Pacific."

"Dream on, Townsend. It's not going to happen."

"Even though it's small, it has everything," he continued, ignoring her protest. "Smooth, sandy beaches, lush greenery, even a waterfall. It's a real paradise."

In spite of herself, Susan could almost see the lovely island in her mind's eye. She pushed the image aside. "It sounds far too remote and primitive for my tastes," she lied.

"You'll change your mind once you see it."

Susan stopped walking. "Listen to me, Hunter. I'm not going to see your island—ever—because the two of us are not getting married."

"How can you say that?" He looked hurt. "We're engaged."

"No, we're not!"

"You still have my ring."

"Only because I forgot to give it back to you yesterday. I'll return it as soon as we get back to the house."

"I don't want it back."

"Too bad," she muttered, shaking her arm loose from his grasp and once more starting out across the front yard. She heard Hunter's squeaking footsteps in the snow behind her as she headed for the porte cochere. She was anxious to see what damage the tree had done to her almost-new car, the convertible she'd bought herself only a few months ago.

From a distance, she thought she noticed a huge branch resting directly atop the car and porte cochere. As she came closer, though, she saw that both were safe.

"You were lucky," Hunter said, echoing her thoughts. "That limb missed doing serious damage by a matter of inches."

Susan nodded. They continued their inspection, walking all the way around the fallen tree. "The tree made a mess out of your driveway," Hunter said. "Aside from that, I can't see that any harm was done."

"My car's trapped inside the porte cochere," she said pointedly.

"Where would you drive if you could get it out? All the streets are impassable by now."

"I suppose you're right," she said. Still, the idea of being *trapped* disturbed her. She shivered as a fierce blast of icy wind hit them. The snow was still falling as heavily as ever, maybe more so.

"We'd better get inside," Hunter suggested.

Susan readily agreed. They started back toward her house but she stopped after a moment. "Did you hear that?"

"What? The wind?" Hunter asked.

"I don't think so. Listen." They both stood still, but all Susan could see was the softly falling snow and all she could hear was the howling wind. "I guess it was nothing," she said, ready to give up.

"Wait!" Hunter commanded. "I heard something, too."

They both listened. They heard the sound again at the same time. "I hear it!" Susan said. "It sounds sort of..."

"Like a cat," Hunter said, finishing her sentence. "I think it came from..."

"Up there!" Susan said, finishing his sentence. She pointed at a tall elm tree a few feet from where they were standing. They moved closer to the tree simultaneously.

"It *is* a cat," he said.

"A kitten," she corrected.

"Half-grown," he amended.

"Poor little thing."

"The noise of the tree falling probably frightened him . . . or her."

"Here, kitty, kitty!" Susan called. The kitten looked at her but didn't budge. "Here, kitty, kitty!" she repeated.

"I don't think he's ready to come down," Hunter commented.

"As cold as it is down here, it's bound to be a lot colder up there," she said.

He shrugged.

"He could freeze!" Susan said.

"I'm sure he'll come down before that happens."

"What if he doesn't?"

"He will."

"You don't know that he will."

"And you don't know that he won't."

"We have to do something," she declared.

"What do you suggest?"

Susan rubbed her arms, trying to stay warm so she could think better. "I wonder if the fire department still rescues cats from high places."

"Even if they did, do you really think they'd have time to spare today, what with all the real emergencies around town?"

"This is a real emergency, too," she said. "But I see what you mean," she added quickly when she saw the look he gave her.

The kitten gave a long, drawn-out *"Me-o-o-w,"* heartbreaking in its intensity. They both looked up at the pitiful little thing high in the elm tree.

"What *can* we do, Hunter?"

He gave a long, drawn-out sigh that oddly reminded Susan of the cat's meow. He unzipped his heavy jacket, took it off and folded it neatly, then handed it to her.

"What are you doing?" she asked.

"You don't expect me to climb a tree in this bulky thing, do you? I'd fall and break my neck before I was halfway up."

"But you shouldn't climb the tree. It's slippery. And the wind's so strong. And—"

"How else do you propose we get the damned cat down?" He started walking toward the tree.

Susan followed right behind him. "Let's wait a little longer and see if he comes down on his own."

"If we wait too long, it'll be dark and I won't be able to climb. And the temperature will drop even lower."

Susan was torn between fear for the cat's safety and fear for Hunter's safety. "Don't do it," she said, placing her hand on his arm to detain him.

He looked at her, his dark eyes unreadable, then he grinned and patted her hand. "Don't worry. I'll be okay. I've been climbing trees since I was barely able to walk."

She was tempted to make a retort about his not being able to walk if he fell and broke his leg, but resisted the temptation. "Be careful," she said, instead.

"You bet," Hunter said, jumping into the air to grab a low-slung branch with his hands, then slinging one leg over the limb to begin his climb.

"You looked like a professional," she said with admiration.

"That was the easy part," he said.

She immediately saw what he meant. Except for that one low limb, there were no more convenient branches for him to grab for quite a distance, so he had to shinny up the main trunk of the tree.

Susan watched from the ground, horror mixed with fascination, as Hunter gradually climbed upward. His progress seemed painfully slow to her, and she was sure it was even more so from his point of view, especially the painful part.

She gasped when he appeared to have lost his grip and slid several feet down the tree. "Are you all right?" she yelled.

She saw him take a deep breath before he replied. "Just a little out of practice."

She was relieved—momentarily—when he reached an area where he could again hold on to branches. Her relief was shattered when he tested one of them and it broke off beneath his weight. Luckily, he still had a tight grip on a sturdier limb. She closed her eyes and kept quiet. She didn't want to say anything that might distract him.

"Here, kitty, kitty."

Susan opened her eyes when she heard Hunter's coaxing voice. He was high in the tree, on the same level as the kitten, who took a step farther out on the branch as she watched.

"Dammit, cat!" Hunter shouted. "Don't make this more difficult than it already is!"

Susan would have laughed if she hadn't been so scared.

"Good kitty," Hunter said, more calmly. "Yes. Good, good kitty. Good kitty's going to let Uncle Hunter rescue him. Yes, he is."

While he was talking in a soothing, singsong voice, Hunter inched toward the cat... closer and closer. Suddenly, his arm shot out and grabbed the animal.

"Gotcha!" he shouted triumphantly.

Susan started breathing again.

"Stop that, dammit!" Hunter shouted.

"What's happening?" she yelled up at him.

"The damned cat's trying to claw me! What an ingrate!"

Susan didn't have a clear view because of the branches in between them, but she saw Hunter start to descend the tree, and figured he must have subdued the animal. She permitted herself a small sigh of relief, which turned out to be premature.

"Susan," Hunter said a moment later. "We have a slight problem here."

He and his captive had reached the part of the tree where there were no branches, the part that Hunter had had to shinny up, holding on to the trunk. "Can I do something to help?" she asked.

"Yes. Unfold my jacket and hold it out underneath me and the cat. I'm going to lean down as far as I can and drop the kitten to you. It's not that big a drop, and shouldn't hurt him. Okay?"

"Okay," she said, unfolding the jacket. She moved to the left, then to the right, then slightly to the left again. "I think I'm directly under you now," she said.

Grasping the kitten with one hand and an overhead branch with the other, Hunter shinnied down the tree as far as he could. He leaned over toward the ground and held out the kitten. "Ready?" he asked.

"Ready."

He dropped the kitten. It made a perfect landing in the outstretched jacket Susan held between her hands. Before Susan could bat an eyelash, the animal bounded off the jacket onto the ground and darted away. She started after it, but stopped when she heard strange noises behind her. She turned just in time to see Hunter tumbling from the tree.

"HUNTER! Are you all right? Hunter, *speak to me!*"

Opening his eyes, he held up his hand to prove to Susan that he was still alive. He'd simply landed on his back and had the breath knocked out of him.

"Hunter, speak to me!" she said again, bringing her face so close to his that he could feel her warm breath against his cold cheeks.

He pointed to his throat, trying to show her that he couldn't talk at the moment.

"Is it your neck?" she asked, tears welling up in her eyes. "Dear Lord, is your neck broken?"

He moved his head from side to side.

She cupped his head between her hands. Her tears dripped onto his face. "What is it, then? Tell me what's wrong!"

"Wind...wind...knocked..."

"Wind knocked out?" she asked. "You had the wind knocked out of you?"

He nodded.

"And that's all?"

He nodded again.

"Thank heavens!" She gave a shaky laugh and cradled his head and shoulders in her arms. "You scared the living daylights out of me."

She hugged him hard, then abruptly released him. "I shouldn't do that."

"What?" he asked.

"I shouldn't squeeze you. I should give you a chance to regain your breath."

"It's okay for you to squeeze me," he said, wishing she would. Her arms were still around him, cradling him against her chest. "I'm better now."

"Do you feel well enough to sit up?" she asked.

Hunter wished that he hadn't said he was better, but it was too late to change his story. "I suppose so."

"I'm worried about your lying on the snow too long and catching cold," Susan said. "You don't even have your jacket."

That reminded him of his reason for climbing the tree in the first place. "What happened to the kitten?"

"He ran away as soon as he touched ground safely. He's an ungrateful cur."

Hunter grinned. "I think a cur is a dog."

"Whatever. He was still ungrateful." Using her arms, she gently but firmly urged him to an upright position.

Hunter reluctantly allowed her to do it. Susan got to her feet and held out her hand to help him up. He took her hand and started to pull himself up. *"Ow!"* he cried out as he felt an excruciating pain in his right ankle. He released her hand and leaned back while he waited for the pain to subside.

"What is it?"

"My ankle," he said. Bending forward, he gingerly touched his ankle, then moved it around. "I don't think it's broken."

"How can you tell?"

Putting all his weight on his good foot, Hunter got up. He draped his arm around Susan's shoulders for support and gradually tested putting a little weight on the injured ankle. "Like this," he said. After a moment, he nodded. "It's only a sprain." He took a step and winced. "Not that it still doesn't hurt like hell."

"Lean on me as much as you can," Susan said.

"Thanks. I intend to."

It was slow going, but they finally made it to Susan's slippery front steps. "If it's all the same to you," Hunter said, "I think I'll crawl the rest of the way."

When he reached the porch, he found that it had become icy, as well, so he crawled across it. Susan held open the front door and Hunter was about to crawl inside the house when something darted past him. "What was that?" he asked Susan as he got to his feet.

"Believe it or not, it was your kitten."

"*My* kitten?"

"You're the one who rescued it, not me," she said. Moving to his side, she took his arm and placed it around her shoulders. She wound her own arm around his waist for added support.

"Are you taking me to my bed?" he asked.

"How about the sofa in the living room, instead?"

"Good choice."

Hunter closed his eyes with relief when he finally settled onto the sofa. His ankle was throbbing relentlessly and he'd broken out in a cold sweat on his forehead and above his upper lip.

"Ow!" he said, opening his eyes again as Susan lifted his foot. He saw her kneeling beside the sofa. "What are you doing?"

"Removing your boot," she replied matter-of-factly.

"Can't you just leave it alone? My ankle hurts when you touch it."

She shook her head. "Imagine how much worse it would hurt if we waited until it was all swollen."

Hunter shuddered at the thought and kept quiet while she took off his boot and sock.

"It's already starting to swell," she said when she finished. "We need to put an ice pack on it. I think I have one in the hall closet."

"Why not just bring in some snow from outside?"

"I can see you're going to be a terrible patient," she said as she got up.

"The worst," he agreed, eyeing her jean-clad rear end with appreciation as she left the room. He smiled, thinking that he'd never considered Susan to be the motherly-nurse type before. And maybe she hadn't been when he first knew her. Two years was a long time.

Out of nowhere, he remembered something her mother had told him over the phone. She'd said that Susan had been devastated when he left two years ago. That was a strong word to use—*devastated*. Not merely sad, unhappy, embarrassed, bummed-out or blue. But *devastated*.

He'd been furious with Susan when he'd called and found out she was engaged to someone else. And he'd been deeply hurt to think that she cared so little for him that she'd forgotten him in such a short time. So it was quite a shock to him to hear that she cared so deeply that she'd been *devastated* when he left. Coming from Mrs. Brantley, who had an excellent command of the English language and didn't tend to exaggerate, *devastated* was a *very* strong word to use. Very strong indeed.

"Here we are," Susan said cheerfully, coming into the living room with an ice bag in one hand and a plump pillow in the other. She moved quickly and efficiently, arranging and rearranging until his ankle was relatively comfortable on the pillow and the ice bag was properly in place.

"There," she said. "Do you need anything else?"

He thought for a moment. "I could do with some dry clothes. I got wet when I pulled off my jacket."

She nodded. "Is there something in particular you want to wear?"

"Anything will do. Just grab the first thing you see."

While Susan was gone, Hunter pulled off his wet sweater and cotton shirt. After hesitating a moment, he took off his undershirt, as well. Then he grinned and lay back on the sofa to wait for Susan to return.

He was rewarded for his efforts by the sight of her eyes widening as soon as she came in and saw him. He had to hand it to her, though. She made an instant recovery, barely missing a beat. She even sat down on the sofa beside him to help him put on the clean sweatshirt she'd brought.

"Here's a towel to dry your hair," she said when the sweatshirt was in place.

"Aren't you going to help me?" he asked.

"Do you need help?"

"Yes." He was watching her intently, willing her to look at him. Finally she did. Their gazes met and held. "Please," he added, his voice barely above a whisper. He saw her rapid intake of breath.

Then she put the towel over his head, covering his eyes, as well. He grinned underneath the towel as she vigorously rubbed his hair, and kept on rubbing.

At last she stopped and removed the towel. "How's that?" she asked, looking at a spot above his head rather than directly at him. He didn't answer and finally she looked into his eyes. He reached up his hand to touch her cheek, caressed it for a moment, then slid his fingers behind her neck and pulled her head down to his. He kissed her.

She briefly resisted. Her hand, trapped between them, pushed against his chest and her lips compressed tightly. Then Hunter felt her hand relax, felt her fingers splay out on his chest and felt her lips soften against his. Her mouth opened and Hunter sought the remembered sweetness inside it, touching and tasting her as if the years had never separated them.

He heard a sound—a moan of pleasure—and didn't know whether it had come from her or himself. It didn't matter. Nothing mattered except the here and now and the two of them together again at last, their lips clinging, breaths intermingling, hearts beating as one. He wanted this moment to last forever.

But of course it didn't. Nothing ever did.

Slowly—and Hunter could swear it was reluctantly—Susan pulled away from him. At least she didn't try to hide her eyes from him. They were a deep green now. Puzzled? Troubled?

"Why did you do that?" she asked breathlessly.

"My way of saying thank-you?" he suggested.

She took a deep breath. "A simple handshake would have been quite sufficient," she said. "And a lot more appropriate."

"Why would it have been more appropriate?" he asked, taking her hand between both of his. She tried to tug it free, but he held on tightly.

"Well . . . I *am* engaged."

"Damned right you are!" he said. "You're engaged to me."

She yanked her hand loose and stood up. "I told you to stop saying that, Hunter."

"I'll never stop saying it, Susan. You…and I…are engaged."

"No, we're not!"

"Then why do you still have my ring?"

"Why do you keep bringing that up?"

"I asked my question first."

"Damn you, Hunter. I'll get the ring right now," she said, starting for the door. "It'll be a pleasure to throw it in your face."

She took another step and the lights went out. Again.

Chapter Nine

"I think they're gone for good this time," Hunter said.

The lights had been off for more than an hour, and Susan was inclined to agree with him. She had already gathered all the candles and flashlights she could find, along with two decorative kerosene lamps. She had placed one lamp in the kitchen and the other on a table in the living room, ready to light when needed. From the looks of things, that could be anytime now.

She had built a fire in the living room fireplace, surprising even herself when it did so well. The fire caught immediately and was now blazing cheerily almost half an hour later. *A good thing, too,* she thought. The temperature inside the house had been dropping steadily since the power went off and the electric thermostat that controlled the heat went with it.

"Maybe I should serve the soup now while it's still warm," Susan said. At Hunter's suggestion, she'd tasted it earlier to see if the peas had cooked long enough. They had. And the soup itself had been surprisingly not bad, pretty good, in fact.

"Good idea," Hunter said, sitting up and swinging his legs off the sofa. He winced when his ankle touched the floor. "I'll come with you."

"You'll do no such thing. I saw you wince."

"Of course you did. My ankle hurts like the devil when I put any weight on it. But I can't lie on your sofa forever."

"I'll tell you what," she said, compromising. "You stay put for now, and I'll look for an elastic bandage after we eat. Okay?"

"I guess it'll have to be," he grumbled, lying back on the sofa once more.

The phone rang when she was on her way out the door. "I'll get it in the kitchen," she told Hunter.

"Ten to one it's that Verner guy again," Hunter yelled after her.

It was.

"Yes, Michael," she said wearily in answer to his first question as to whether Hunter was still there.

"Honestly, Susan," he said, sounding as exasperated as she was beginning to feel, "I'm disappointed in you. Kenneth and I both agree that Townsend is taking advantage of you."

"You've been discussing me with my stepfather?" she asked incredulously.

"Only because we both care about you. We're concerned about you and your reputation."

"Thanks for caring, Michael," she responded angrily. "But I can handle my own reputation. It's my business and not yours."

"I don't see it that way. After all, you *are* my fiancée."

"And you're mine. But I don't tell you who you can have as a guest in your own home."

"Neither would I, ordinarily. But Townsend is a different case."

"Because we used to be engaged?"

"It's not just that," Michael said self-righteously.

"What exactly is it, then?"

"You have to be firm with people like Townsend. Simply put your foot down and tell him to leave."

"I don't think he could do that. He came by taxi and they aren't running anymore except for extreme emergencies."

"He could take public transit."

"There's a problem with that, too," she said. "The nearest bus stop is several blocks from my house and Hunter could never walk that far."

"Why not? He seemed healthy enough to me."

"That was day before yesterday, and he was healthy then. But today he sprained his ankle and can barely walk."

"He's probably faking."

"No. I saw him fall out of the tree myself."

"What the devil was he doing up in a tree?"

"He was rescuing a kitten."

"What kitten?"

"How should I know? It was a kitten from the neighborhood. It must have run up the tree because it was frightened. It wouldn't come down, so Hunter climbed up and rescued it."

She waited for Michael's response, but heard only silence. "Michael? Are you still there?"

"I'm here. I'm thinking."

That's always a bad sign, she thought uncharitably.

"If Townsend can't or won't leave your house," he said after several moments, "then perhaps you should leave."

"What?"

"You could crank up your BMW... it has excellent traction and steering. You could drive over to my place. What do you think?"

"I think you've lost your mind."

"Seriously, Susan. You should be able to make the drive in no time. It's a straight shot, all level ground once you hit Peachtree Road."

Susan could hardly believe what she was hearing. Michael had refused to drive to her house this morning, when the roads were in much better shape than they were now. Yet he was so jealous of Hunter that he had the nerve to suggest she risk life and limb to drive to his house now!

With extreme effort, she fought back the urge to tell him what she thought of him *and* his stupid idea. "There's a problem with that, too, Michael," she said, instead. "Remember my neighbor's huge oak tree, the one you admired so much?"

"Of course."

"It fell across my yard a little while ago."

"Good Lord!"

Susan smiled with satisfaction. "Yes. It missed my house by a matter of inches, but the driveway's completely blocked."

"Why didn't you tell me this before?"

You were so busy running your own mouth that you didn't give me a chance to tell you, she thought. "I'm telling you now."

"Are you all right?"

That was the question you should have asked in the first place, she thought. "I'm fine."

"I, uh, suppose you won't be able to leave your house anytime soon."

"It sure seems that way."

"Is there anything I can do?"

He was asking all the right questions now, but as far as she was concerned, it was way too late. "Not that I know of."

"Well, uh...call me if...you know."

"Of course. Goodbye, Michael."

Susan stood by the phone for a long time after she'd hung up, rehashing the conversation. Then she shook her head, walked over to the sink and thoroughly washed her hands.

After she'd finished, she washed them again. She wondered briefly if the action was symbolic.

She didn't like what she was thinking.

But she couldn't help thinking it.

Had she made a mistake—a truly terrible mistake—in becoming engaged to Michael Verner?

HUNTER SIGHED with satisfaction as he finished the last of his soup. "A truly memorable meal," he said.

Susan laughed. "Hodgepodge soup made with leftover peas from New Year's is *memorable?*"

"Well, of course the ambience added to the pleasure of the meal," he observed, sweeping out his hand in an expansive gesture. He was seated on the sofa in the living room—as always—and she sat cross-legged on the floor across the coffee table from him. The kitten he'd rescued earlier was curled on the sofa beside him.

On his left, a cheery fire crackled in the fireplace. The outdoorsy aroma of burning wood mingled with the spicy-sweet odor of scented oil burning in the lamp and wax from the single candle Susan had placed in a silver holder on the coffee table.

"But as you know, presentation is everything," he continued. "And yours was superb, Susan." In addition to candlelight, she had provided decorative place mats, fine china, linen napkins and silver service, as well as vintage wine in crystal goblets.

"To a marvelous hostess," Hunter said, raising his wineglass in a toast.

She acknowledged his toast with a semi-curtsy from her seated position. Hunter didn't know how she'd managed it, but laughed with pleasure. God, she was beautiful tonight! And delightful. She'd kept him entertained throughout dinner with outrageous tales from "the wonderful world of advertising," as she phrased it.

It had been a long, long time since he'd enjoyed a woman's company as much as he had enjoyed Susan's this evening. The wine and the sense of isolation—as if the two of them were alone on a deserted island—might have had something to do with his feeling. But there was more to it than that, he knew.

He was afraid there was much more to it than that.

"Your mother told me something interesting on the phone today," he said.

The flickering firelight made Susan's smile enigmatic. She tilted her head to one side in a gesture he remembered well. "And what was that?"

"She said you were devastated when I left."

The smile disappeared completely. She looked as if she'd just been slapped.

"What would you expect?" she asked tersely. "I was young. And I thought I was in love."

"Do you still?" When she looked perplexed, he added, "Think you were in love with me back then, I mean."

She didn't speak for so long that he thought she might not answer at all.

"Yes."

Hunter blinked. "I'm sorry I hurt you, Susan."

"Thank you."

"I never meant to hurt you." That was true. He'd believed he was dying and had been trying to save her, not hurt her.

"It wasn't your fault."

She was thinking about the amnesia—she finally believed he'd actually had a loss of memory. *Damn!* Even though he'd had what he thought was a compelling reason to leave her—desert her—the fact remained that he'd known exactly what he was doing at the time. It *was* his fault.

"I was surprised to learn that your mother and stepfather were divorced," he said, changing the subject.

"Yes. It came as a surprise to me, too."

"Do you think their split had anything to do with me?"

"You?" she asked. "Why would it?"

"I don't know... But I know your mother liked me and he hated me."

Susan shook her head. "You'd been gone a long time when they decided to divorce. They had no reason to disagree about you."

Hunter took a sip of his wine. As soon as he'd learned he didn't have a brain tumor, the first thing he did was place a telephone call to Susan. He'd talked to her stepfather, who'd promised to relay his message... but of course never did.

He thought it significant that a maid rather than her husband had told Helen Brantley that Hunter had phoned, trying to get in touch with Susan. It was especially significant in light of the fact that the Brantleys' divorce took place shortly after that.

He couldn't voice his suspicions to Susan, though, without disclosing that he'd tried to call her eighteen months after he left. That, in turn, would reveal that he hadn't had amnesia then. Was he ready to tell her the truth?

Susan had finally accepted his lie. They were almost close to being friends again. What would her reaction be if he told her the truth—the whole truth?

She'd been furious when he'd mentioned her stepfather in connection with his suspicions about his headaches. How would she feel about a false diagnosis of a brain tumor?

He honestly didn't know. He debated with himself, and finally decided not to risk telling her... not quite yet.

"I think you were right about one thing, Hunter," Susan said, interrupting his thoughts.

"What's that?"

"I think Kenneth does hate you...much more than I ever dreamed."

Her bald statement caught him completely by surprise. "I, uh, what made you come to that conclusion?"

Susan hesitated, as if trying to determine what or how much to tell him. Hunter kept quiet. He wanted to give her plenty of time, as much as she needed.

"He called me today," she finally said.

The phone call that upset her so much this morning! Hunter thought. So he'd been right, after all, in deciding it was Brantley who'd made it.

"What did he say?" Hunter asked, trying to sound calm.

"Michael had told him you were here, which I thought was a little strange," she said.

More than a little, Hunter thought.

"I can't remember Kenneth's exact words, but much of what he said was uncomplimentary to you— things he's said before. Things *I've* said before," she added, looking directly into his eyes.

"I understand," Hunter said.

"So it wasn't so much what he said as the way he said it. He's usually the one person you can count on to be calm in any situation. But today, he was so upset, he was beside himself. He was actually shouting."

"I don't know him as well as you do," Hunter commented, "but it does seem out of character."

"It is," Susan said. "I've never known him to be so agitated. Or so... vehement."

"Can you remember *anything* specific that he said?"

"Well, he called you a liar." She lifted one eyebrow. "But as you know, I've called you that myself."

"I know," he said, forcing a smile.

"He told me not to believe anything you said...that it was only your desperate attempt to confuse me."

"Anything else?" Hunter asked. His heart was pounding furiously after Susan's last revelation.

She thought some more and then shook her head. "The rest was mostly variations on the same theme, except he did seem to think it was imperative that I get you out of my house as quickly as possible."

Of course Brantley wants me out of her house,
Hunter thought. *He's afraid I might tell her all I know
and suspect about him. And more than that, he's
afraid she might start to believe me!*

He took another sip of wine. Maybe it was time he
exposed Susan to the whole story, after all.

"Like I said before, the entire conversation was totally unlike Kenneth," she said.

"At least some good came out of it," Hunter told
her.

"Oh?"

"You've finally conceded that I was correct all
along—Brantley hates me with a passion."

"I suppose," she agreed with a rueful smile. "If you
call that a good thing."

"It's a start."

She narrowed her eyes. "A start...leading to
what?"

"Suppose, just suppose, that Brantley hated me
enough to send me to a quack two years ago."

"Dr. Estep, I presume."

"Right."

"With what purpose in mind?"

"That Dr. Estep would say or do something that
would harm rather than help me."

Susan shook her head. "So we're back to the poison pills again."

"Maybe Brantley merely hoped that Dr. Estep
would...make a wrong diagnosis or something.
Anything that would cause me to fear for my health
and possibly postpone our marriage because of it."

"But that didn't happen," she said. "Unless... Are
you suggesting that the pills Dr. Estep gave you
brought on your amnesia, too?"

Hunter had started to sweat. Profusely. He wasn't sure where he was heading in this conversation.

"I don't know what I'm suggesting, Susan," he said truthfully. "I only know that *something* happened to me two years ago. I'd like to talk to Dr. Estep in person to find out if he can shed any light on the situation."

She studied his face intently, her eyes unreadable. Finally, she nodded. "That sounds reasonable enough. As long as your main purpose is merely to talk with him, and not make any wild accusations."

He held up his right hand in the Boy Scouts' salute. "That's all I want to do—talk with him."

"Then you should do it. By all means."

"There's a problem with that. I can't find him in the Atlanta phone directory. I've looked under every category I can think of, and called information at least ten times. I simply can't find him."

"Perhaps he's retired."

"He's not old enough to retire."

"Maybe he's dead."

"That's a possibility. But I'd like to know for sure."

She narrowed her eyes again. "And you want me to help you find out. You want me to ask Kenneth."

Hunter grinned with profound relief. "How did you guess?"

"How could I not guess?"

"Will you do it?" He watched her fiddle with her wineglass while he waited for her response.

"I'd rather not call him tonight," she finally said.

"Tomorrow would be fine."

"Very well. I'll do it."

Hunter let out the breath he'd been holding. "Thank you, Susan," he said.

"You're welcome." She pushed up from the floor and got to her feet in one graceful movement. She started stacking dishes onto a tray.

Feeling decidedly *not* graceful, Hunter got up, too. The kitten opened its eyes and gave him an indignant stare. "Don't worry, cat," he said. "I'll be back as soon as I wash the dishes."

"There's no need for that. I'll load them in..." She stopped in midsentence and made a face. "The dishwasher operates on electricity."

"Which we don't have," he said, finishing her thought. He hobbled a couple of steps. "Do you have an umbrella or something I could use as a walking stick?"

"I have better than that," Susan replied. "I don't know why I didn't think of it before."

She left the room. The kitten looked at Hunter and meowed. "I don't know why you're complaining," he told it. "Susan said you ate almost a whole jar of smoked oysters."

"Ta-da!" Susan said, coming into the living room with a wooden cane in her hand. She grinned as she held it out to Hunter.

It took him a moment to recognize the cane and understand the reason for her grin. "This is the walking stick I won for you at the state fair years ago!"

She nodded. "The very same."

"I can't believe you kept it all this time."

She shrugged, and suddenly looked shy. "I thought it might come in handy sometime."

"It certainly did!" he said, testing the cane. "This is wonderful . . . just perfect," he added, hobbling off to the kitchen.

"I GUESS that's everything," Susan said, turning back the covers and plumping the pillows on the sofa one last time. She stood up straight and looked at Hunter, who'd just returned to the living room. He was fully dressed, but his hair was still wet from the shower. She could swear he'd shaved, too, and wondered if he always did that in preparation for bed.

It was time she got ready for bed, too.

The dishes were washed and dried, the kitten was settled into a cozy box next to the hot-water heater in the pantry and she'd hauled out all the warm bed covers she could find. Unfortunately, she'd already stored most of the winter blankets. By all rights, the weather should be too warm now to need them.

"Are you sure you'll be comfortable sleeping on the sofa?" she asked Hunter.

"A lot more comfortable than I'd be in that ice-cold bedroom. At least the fireplace takes the chill off the room."

He moved toward her, favoring his sprained ankle but managing the cane quite well, she thought. As if by reflex, she took a step backward.

He smiled. "Why don't you join me on the sofa? There's plenty of room."

She shook her head. "No, thanks."

"I don't see any good reason why you won't," he said, moving closer still, until he was standing so close she could smell his after-shave lotion.

Susan could think of a dozen reasons, but one was more than enough—Hunter himself. He was too damned attractive for his own good, and for hers. "I'm not going to sleep with you, Hunter."

"It's a long sofa. We could sleep toe to toe and keep our feet warm."

"No, Hunter."

He gave a long, exaggerated sigh, then reached out to touch her cheek, moving his fingers lightly along her skin and giving her goose bumps. "In that case, I guess I'll have to settle for a good-night kiss."

Thinking of the last time they'd kissed, her lips twitched involuntarily. "Not that, either," she said.

"Just a little peck on the cheek?" he coaxed.

His lips were mere inches from her eyes and Susan couldn't tear her gaze away from them. They were smooth and pink, invitingly kissable. "If that's all," she conceded, knowing she shouldn't but ignoring the warning signals going off inside her.

He nodded and touched his mouth to her cheek. His lips were infinitely soft, just as she remembered them. And warm. She felt his breath on her cheek as his mouth opened, felt the touch of his tongue as well as his lips as they moved slowly toward her mouth, closer and closer, teasing her with their touch, tempting her with their warmth. She closed her eyes.

At the last moment—when she had already decided she wouldn't stop him if he tried to kiss her mouth— his lips moved away, sliding across her cheek toward her ear. Heaven forbid! Hunter knew how she reacted to a kiss on the ear.

He knew very well. Opening her eyes, she pushed him away. Sure enough, he was grinning. She shook her head and grinned back at him. "You dirty rat," she whispered tenderly, moving her hand to caress his cheek this time.

"It was just a peck on the cheek," he said innocently.

"Indeed." Surprised at her own reluctance to move away from him, she forced herself. "Good night, Hunter," she said as she started out of the room.

"If your bed's too cold, remember there's always a warm place here," he called after her.

Susan took a hot shower, then hurried to bed before its effects could wear off. The sheets were cold as ice, and she smiled again as she recalled Hunter's parting words. She burrowed down under the covers—what few there were—still thinking about him.

She was glad they were on better terms with each other now, more relaxed—friendly, although she knew they could never be friends. There was too much history between them for that.

She'd almost forgotten how much fun he was to be around. He still liked to tease, just as he always had. But now there was a serious side to him, too, that hadn't been there before.

Susan shivered. It really was cold in here, and her bed didn't seem to be warming up the way it should. She tried to forget it, and thought about Hunter again. At least she didn't hate him anymore. She wondered if she really ever had. She'd been wounded by a hurt that went so deep, it was hard to tell where it left off and other emotions took over.

She shivered again. She wondered what Hunter thought about the past—their past—now that he could recall it again. She honestly didn't know. In some ways, she knew him so well. In others, she didn't know him at all . . . he was a total stranger.

That wasn't surprising. He'd been younger when he went away, of course. Now he was more of a man— very much so—and secure in his own masculinity. How many men did she know who would take over the cooking chores in a woman's kitchen the way Hunter had done this morning!

He'd even made oatmeal, for heaven's sake! She giggled. Then she shivered.

She doubted that many men would have been soft-hearted enough to risk life and limb to rescue a helpless kitten, either, as Hunter had done today.

She certainly couldn't imagine Michael doing it. He'd refused to drive to her house in the snow, even though he was alarmed because she and Hunter were home alone. Then, instead of coming to her rescue, he'd had the nerve to suggest that she crank up her car and drive to *his* apartment!

By now, Susan was shivering so hard, her teeth were chattering. She wasn't sure whether it was because of the cold or because she was furious and disgusted with Michael. Possibly, it was both.

Either way, she couldn't stand it anymore. She had to do something. Maybe another hot shower would help. She threw back the thin covers and got out of bed. Pausing only long enough to pull on her robe and bedroom slippers, she padded to the door and threw it open.

Hunter was standing in the hallway just outside her door. He had a blanket wrapped around him. "What are you doing up?" he demanded.

"I'm freezing," she admitted.

"I know."

"How did you know? And what are you doing here outside my door?"

"I was cold, too, even with the fireplace. I figured you must have turned into an icicle by now. I came to rescue you."

"How?"

"You were right about the sofa," he said. "It's too small for both of us, so we'll share your bed. I even brought my own blanket."

Chapter Ten

"Y-you can't do that," Susan stammered. "I mean . . . we can't share a bed."

"Don't be Victorian about this, Suse," Hunter said. "It has nothing to do with sex, lust or public opinion. It's a matter of survival."

"It's not *that* cold."

"Maybe not, but it feels like it is. At the very least, it's cold enough to keep us awake all night."

"I'd planned to take another hot shower," she said.

Hunter could tell she was wavering. "The effects of that will only last a little while. Then you'll be colder than ever."

"If I agree to this—and that's a big if—do you promise you won't try anything?"

"I promise I won't try *any*thing. I just want to get warm enough to get some sleep."

She glanced down at his feet. One was bare and the other was partially wrapped in an elastic bandage. She looked back to his face again with a frown. "Do you have any clothes on underneath that blanket?"

With a flourish and a grin, Hunter suddenly flung out his arms.

Susan gaped. "Long johns?"

"Thermal underwear," he corrected.

"You can close your blanket now," she said quickly. "I merely asked a question. I didn't expect a...a demonstration."

"I'm always happy to oblige—anything to put your mind at rest," he said. "And now that you see I'm fully clothed, neck to ankle, can we go to bed before we both catch pneumonia?"

"I suppose so," she finally agreed.

Hunter brushed past her and hobbled to the bed before she could change her mind. He spread his blanket on top of her covers. "Which side do you sleep on?" he asked matter-of-factly.

Susan pointed to the left side. Hunter nodded and quickly got into her bed on the right side, pulling the covers up over his head in case she felt shy about removing her robe in front of him. "You'd better hurry to bed before you get any colder," he called from underneath the covers.

After a moment, he heard the rustle of her movements and then felt the bed give as she got into it.

Hunter counted to a hundred before he sneaked his head out from under the covers. His eyes had adjusted to the darkness by then, and he could see the outline of Susan's body huddled on the far side of the bed, at the very edge.

He smiled. "Be careful," he whispered. "You could fall off."

"I'm fine," she mumbled.

"No you're not. I can feel the bed move with your shivering."

"It'll stop after a while."

"It'll stop a lot quicker if you move over this way...close enough so that our bodies are touching."

"Absolutely not."

"We'd generate more heat if we were touching," he told her reasonably. "It would make us both warm."

"Forget it."

"I don't see why you're being so stubborn about this. Are you afraid of me?"

"Of course not!" she protested.

"I already promised I wouldn't try anything."

"What do you call what you're suggesting?"

"I call it trying to keep warm. That's all. We could sleep spoon-style—my front to your back or vice versa. Whichever you prefer."

"And that's all?"

"Absolutely."

"Okay, then." She rolled over onto her side, facing him.

"No," he said. "You're colder, so let's do it the opposite way to begin with."

When she started to turn onto her other side, he reached out his arm to pull her close to the center of the bed.

"What are you doing!" she exclaimed.

"I'm trying to keep you from falling off the damned bed. That's *all!*" He moved close behind her, until their bodies were touching. "God, you have a suspicious mind."

He kept his right arm draped across her. His left arm was trapped between them, but he didn't dare do anything about it at the moment.

"Now," he said, moving his hips until he was comfortably pressed against her backside. "Try to relax and get some sleep."

"That's easy for you to say."

"I don't see why you're so uptight. It's not as if I could actually *do* anything, what with that heavy-gauge flannel nightgown you're wearing. Even if I wanted to . . . which I don't," he added.

"Just shut up, Hunter."

He grinned. After all, he'd accomplished what he'd set out to do, hadn't he? He *had* been a little chilly on the sofa, but only a little, not nearly enough to keep him awake. However, he'd known that Susan had to be much colder than he was, since he'd noticed her giving him the lion's share of the covers.

Stubborn Susan would never admit her discomfort to him, so he'd forced the issue by pretending to be miserably cold himself. He'd been almost certain she would take pity on him and allow him into her bed.

His plan had worked like a charm. He'd be able to take care of her tonight, making sure she was warm and comfortable.

He felt her shivering gradually subside. The tension left her body, too, and her breathing became slow and regular as she drifted toward sleep.

Perversely, the more she relaxed—the more the soft warmth of her body heated him wherever they touched—the more his own body tensed. He hadn't counted on that. He'd forgotten how susceptible he was to Susan, to the sight and smell and sound and feel of her.

He carefully inched his hips away from her, temporarily relieving the pressure on that part of him most affected by her closeness.

Susan was sleeping soundly now. She was safe and secure, just as he'd planned. On the other hand, he could already tell that it was going to be a long, long night for him.

And you have only yourself to blame, Townsend, he thought.

SUSAN WAS HAVING the most deliciously erotic dream of her life. Hunter had finally returned to her after a long and almost unbearably painful absence. They'd had a joyous reunion during which they both laughed and cried at the same time. And then they'd been married at the Cathedral of St. Phillip, which had been closed all the years he'd been away but had been reopened for the occasion of their wedding.

Hunter had looked dashingly, dangerously handsome in his black tuxedo, and Susan had worn a white wedding dress that was left over from some other occasion... she couldn't recall what that occasion was.

And now, after all the years and tears and heartbreak, they were on their honeymoon. Hunter's dark eyes gazed deeply into hers, and then he lifted her into his arms—as if she were something very precious, and weighed no more than a doll—and carried her to their marriage bed.

He kissed her, every part of her, tenderly at first, then with mounting intensity. His kisses set her on fire and she tightened her arms around him. She wanted him more than she'd ever dreamed she could want someone. She was on fire with wanting him... but something was in the way. It was her long wedding dress coming between them, keeping her from him. She tried to push it away, but there was so much of it.

She tightened her arms around him, straining toward him. She felt the heat of his arousal pressing against her, but the damned dress was in the way and she couldn't take him inside her as she ached to do. She moaned with frustration....

Susan opened her eyes.

She closed them and then quickly opened them again. She swallowed. She'd been dreaming about Hunter, but this was no dream. That was Hunter's face barely an inch from hers on the pillow. His eyes were closed, so he must be asleep. It was a good thing he was, too, because she wouldn't want him to know she'd moved so close to him during the night.

Fully awake now, she realized the situation was even worse than she'd first thought. In their sleep, she and Hunter had become a tangle of arms and legs—all of which were situated where they shouldn't be at all. His arm was around her waist, his other hand cupped her breast and one of his legs had insinuated itself intimately between hers.

Her own arm was around his shoulders, her nightgown was up around her waist and her leg was flung across his hips to... *Oh, dear Lord!* That was no dream, either. It was Hunter's real flesh, rock-hard and hot, that she felt pressing against her.

In spite of herself, Susan suddenly felt a fierce rush of desire for that flesh. What kind of weak, wicked creature was she?

She snatched her arm back and tried to move her leg, but the bed covers were tangled, holding her leg firmly in place around his hips. She yanked at the covers, but they wouldn't budge.

Hunter opened his eyes.

"Oh, hell!" she said.

He blinked. "That's quite a greeting."

"Just help me get the cover untangled," she said fiercely.

"Sure." He moved his arm and his eyes widened. "Oh."

He slightly moved his leg—the one that was trapped between her thighs—and his eyes opened even wider. "Oh, my," he said, breaking into a grin.

Well, what had she expected? That he wouldn't notice the intimacy of their entanglement? "Are you going to help me or not?" she asked.

"I'm going to help...but I have a question," he added softly, moving his hand to her hip in an even more intimately suggestive gesture. "How best *can* I help?"

"Not that way," she said, angrily shoving his hand aside.

He chuckled. But at least he finally aided her in getting the covers untangled. As soon as she was set free, Susan started to get out of bed. At the last moment, she remembered to pull down her nightgown first.

Hunter leaned back against the pillows with his arms propped behind his head. There was a hint of a smile at his lips, as if to announce to her and the world at large that he was all male and proud of it.

In spite of his macho posture—or perhaps because of it—Susan felt another surge of raw longing. *Pure animal lust,* she thought, irritated not with him but with herself.

"You needn't look so self-satisfied," she said, pulling on her robe.

"Who, me?" he asked innocently. "I didn't do anything."

It was true. Judging by the final positions of their entanglement in bed, she'd definitely been the aggressor.

"Never mind," she said, gathering fresh clothes to carry to the bathroom with her. She heard him chuckle again as she stalked out the bedroom door.

BY THE TIME Susan had showered and dressed, she felt much better, almost in control of herself again. Almost. She still cringed at the idea of facing Hunter.

At least the snow had stopped. In fact, the day was gorgeous—blue, blue skies and brilliant sunshine that reflected off the snow and made the day even brighter.

Putting on a last touch of lipstick, Susan took a deep breath and marched to her bedroom, half expecting to find Hunter still in bed. He was gone. So was the blanket he'd brought with him, but the rest of the bed was a shambles.

With flaming cheeks, she changed the sheets and made the bed, finishing in record time. When she was done, she headed for the kitchen.

It was cold and empty, and would have been dark if it hadn't been for the bright sunshine streaming in through the window over the sink. Susan walked over to the pantry where she'd made a bed for the kitten. It was empty, too. Taking a deep breath, she made her way to the living room.

He was kneeling in front of the fireplace and the kitten was right beside him, rubbing against his thigh. Hunter wore her cooking mitt on his hand and was holding a saucepan close to the fire, trying to hold it over the flames.

"What—"

He jumped at the sound of her voice, sloshing liquid onto the mitt. "Damn!" he muttered. "Don't ask," he said, giving her the briefest of glances before turning his attention back to the saucepan. After a moment, he put the pan down on the hearth, took off the mitt and blew on his hand, obviously trying to cool it.

"I'm boiling coffee—or trying to—so no snide remarks, please," he said without looking at her.

His ill humor cheered her immediately. "I think I have some long-handled barbecue tongs on the back porch," she said.

He scowled at her. "Why didn't you say so before?"

"You didn't ask me," she replied airily. "I'll be right back."

The tongs were exactly where she'd thought they were—surprise, surprise—and they worked like a charm. When the coffee was made, she helped Hunter pour it through a strainer and into their mugs.

"It's the best coffee I've ever tasted," she declared with conviction after taking a sip.

"I'll bet you say that to all the guys who singe their arm hairs making coffee for you," Hunter countered.

They both laughed, then savored the rest of their coffee in silence. After they finished, Hunter fed the kitten the rest of the jar of smoked oysters while Susan went to make her phone call to her stepfather. She didn't relish the idea of talking to him after yesterday, but a promise was a promise.

"Kenneth? It's Susan," she said when he answered the phone.

"Is something wrong?" he asked, urgency shading his voice.

"No. At least, nothing new. The power's out, and a big tree fell across my driveway yesterday, but I imagine Michael's already told you that."

"Yes, he told me. I suppose that means Townsend's still there."

"Yes," she said, relieved that he couldn't know how much a presence Hunter was in her life or what had been going on between the two of them, particularly in bed this morning. "But the weather is so beautiful today, I imagine the snow will melt and he'll be leaving soon."

Actually, she had no idea when Hunter might leave. Telling her stepfather that it would probably be soon was an outright lie. She was amazed that the fib had come so easily to her lips.

"Good," he said. "The sooner that man is out of your house, the better."

"Yes," she agreed, lying again. It was even easier this time. "And that reminds me. Before he leaves, he asked me to try to get Dr. Estep's address from you."

Susan held her breath and waited, but there was only silence at the other end. "Kenneth, are you still there?" she asked after a moment.

"Yes. I'm here. I was trying to place the name. What was it again?"

"Dr. Estep. Wayne Estep."

"It doesn't ring a bell. Sorry."

Susan's mouth was suddenly dry. "He's the man you referred Hunter to for a physical before . . . before we were supposed to be married."

"I did?" he asked, sounding genuinely surprised.

"Surely you remember."

"Actually, I don't remember. But I'm sure I must have done it . . . if *you* say I did."

Susan swallowed. "Try to think back, Kenneth."

"I've already done that!" he said angrily. "I told you, I don't remember the man. Are you calling me a liar?"

"Of course not!"

"What the hell has Townsend been telling you?"

"Nothing. I—"

"And why does he want to see this doctor in the first place?"

"I . . . I think he just wants to talk to him."

"About what?"

"I'm not sure. Look, Kenneth," she said quickly, "it's probably not that important. I'm sorry I upset you."

She heard him take a deep breath.

"I'm better now," he said finally. "It was just…the idea that you'd think I lied . . ."

"I know," she said. "I'm truly sorry, Kenneth."

"You're forgiven." He sighed. "And if Townsend is so fired up to talk to this doctor, why doesn't he simply look in the telephone book?"

"He did. Dr. Estep isn't listed. And I remembered that you'd been to see Dr. Estep yourself a number of times, so I said I'd ask if you knew how to get in touch with him."

He laughed. "You know how many doctors I see, Susan. How could you possibly expect me to remember one from years ago?"

She forced a laugh, too. "It was a bit ridiculous."

"Sorry I couldn't help you."

"It's okay. Thanks, anyway."

"Call me again if you need anything," he said. "The bank's sending a limo for me, so I'll be at work this afternoon. Then I'll be back here tonight."

"I'll remember. Goodbye, Kenneth."

"Goodbye, Susan."

Susan gently replaced the phone and then closed her eyes. She took several deep breaths before she opened her eyes again and went to tell Hunter the news.

"Well?" he asked as soon as she entered the living room.

"Kenneth said he didn't remember Dr. Estep."

Hunter made a face. "Damn. I was hoping—"

"He was lying," she said softly.

HUNTER STARED at Susan. Her expressive face was void of its usual animation, and her green eyes were filled with infinite sorrow. He remembered once again how much she cared for Kenneth Brantley, who'd been like a father to her since she was a teenager.

"Maybe you're mistaken," he said, hoping to ease her sadness.

"No. There's no mistake."

"But why would he lie?"

"I'm not sure," she said, frowning as she considered the question. "I would guess that it's because he doesn't want you to talk to Dr. Estep."

A chill ran up Hunter's spine. He tried to control his excitement. "How can you be so sure he's lying?"

"It's not one thing in particular," she said. "Just everything in general. His reactions didn't ring true. And also he said he didn't remember Dr. Estep's name."

"Perhaps he really didn't remember the name."

Susan shook her head. "He keeps a written record of every doctor who's ever treated him—names, dates, results—the works."

"Addresses, too?" Hunter asked, his heart racing faster.

"Certainly..." She narrowed her eyes. "What are you thinking, Hunter?"

"This written record of doctors...where does Brantley keep it?"

"In his desk at home. He... Oh, no!"

"What?"

"No, I'm not going to do what you were going to suggest."

"What was I going to suggest?" he asked, trying to sound innocent.

"That I sneak a look at Kenneth's records and get Dr. Estep's address for you."

Hunter shook his head. "You're way off base."

"I am?"

"Yes. I was going to suggest that *we* sneak a look at your stepfather's records."

"No. Absolutely not."

"Why?"

"It's way too risky. There's nothing Kenneth would like more than to have you thrown in jail."

"It won't happen," he said. "The way I figure it, he'll be furious when I waltz into his home with you. We'll argue a bit, and then I'll pretend to leave. While you're still talking to him—keeping him busy—I'll sneak back in and search his desk."

Susan laughed.

"What's wrong with the plan?" he asked, offended.

"Only about a million things." She hesitated. "Besides, there's an easier way."

"What is it?"

"He's not going to be home this afternoon, and I have a key to his house."

This time, Hunter laughed...with relief. "Were you planning to share this crucial information with me?"

"Maybe," she replied. "Or maybe not."

"We still have a problem getting to and from his house. I doubt that a taxi would wait for us, especially since we don't know how long our search will take."

"Yeah," Susan agreed, using a mock-tough tone. "And waiting for another cab would really be a bummer if we have to make a fast getaway."

"Be serious. What we really need to do is find some way to clear the driveway so we can use your car. You don't happen to have a chain saw, do you?"

"No. But my next-door neighbors do."

"Don't tell me, let me guess. You have a key to their house while they're on vacation."

She nodded. "And a key to their garage, where they keep the saw. But will you be able to operate it?" she asked, pointing to his ankle.

In his excitement, Hunter had forgotten about the sprain. "Sure," he replied confidently. "No problem."

THE CHAIN SAW sputtered and died. Again.

"What's wrong now?" Susan asked.

"The wood's so hard, it's causing the teeth to jam," Hunter muttered, feeling a sharp pain in his back as he stood up straight to wipe the sweat off his forehead. *Just one damned problem after another,* he thought.

Simply maneuvering down Susan's slippery front steps with his bum ankle and then through deep drifts of snow to get to the tree had been a huge problem.

The walking cane was useless in the snow, so he'd had to hobble along on his own, falling several times en route.

At least the snow was soft. The kitten loved it. So did Susan, who laughed and played with the kitten when she wasn't busy hauling away limbs as Hunter trimmed them in order to get to the trunk of the tree—the part that was blocking the driveway.

She poured him a cup of water from the thermos she'd brought outside.

"Thanks," he said, accepting the water and drinking thirstily. He smiled at her, and she returned the smile.

The two of them had come a long way in the past couple of days. She'd been wonderful...was still wonderful. Teasing or serious, laughing or sad, tender or testy, she was everything he'd always admired in a woman, everything he'd always wanted. And she was sexy as hell. The memory of her as she'd been in bed this morning flashed through his mind.

He wondered if he was falling in love with her again. He wondered if he'd ever stopped loving her in the first place.

"You're making great progress," Susan said, interrupting his thoughts.

"It's going a little slower than I'd hoped," he replied, looking at the remains of the huge tree. He'd finally cleared away enough limbs to reach the trunk, but had barely made a dent in it.

"You'll get there. You always were impatient, Hunter," she said, giving him a look he couldn't interpret.

Was he? And was there a hidden meaning to her words?

Hunter finished the water and started the chain saw again, still wondering.

He worked steadily for almost an hour, stopping only long enough to remove his sweater and tie a handkerchief around his forehead in lieu of a sweatband. He waved to Susan, who was shoveling snow from the driveway and had almost reached the street. The kitten kept running back and forth between the two of them.

At last, Hunter shut off the chain saw and massaged his aching back while he surveyed his handiwork. He had sawed the tree trunk all the way through in several places. With the exception of one section that was larger than the others, he and Susan should be able to roll the pieces clear of the driveway with no trouble.

He was debating whether to saw the questionable section in half—another twenty or thirty minutes' work—when Susan came up the driveway accompanied by a man and a young boy. In his arms, the boy was carrying the kitten Hunter had rescued.

Susan put her hand on the boy's shoulder when they reached Hunter. "Here he is, Brandon," she said. "This is the nice man who rescued Fluffy for you."

Nice man? Hunter raised his eyebrows as he looked at Susan. *Fluffy?*

She winked at him. "These are my neighbors, Lionel Richards and his son, Brandon. And Hunter Townsend is the man you should thank, Brandon. Not me."

"Thank you," the boy said with a broad smile that revealed two missing front teeth.

"You're wel—"

"The whole family thanks you," Lionel Richards interjected, grabbing Hunter's hand and pumping it enthusiastically. "Brandon was beside himself with grief when Fluffy scooted out the door yesterday and we couldn't find him. Would you believe I was out half the night looking for the da—" He stopped abruptly in midsentence. "For the *dear* cat," he corrected himself with a self-conscious laugh.

"I'm glad I was able to help," Hunter said, feeling self-conscious himself.

"I can't thank you enough," Lionel said. "I wish there was some way to repay you."

"Well, as a matter of fact, there is," Hunter said, suddenly seeing the solution to his problem with the large section of tree trunk.

After Hunter and Lionel cleared all remnants of the tree from Susan's driveway, there were several more rounds of thank-yous. Then the twosome finally left.

"Whew!" Susan said when they were out of earshot.

Hunter turned to her. "Fluffy?" he said.

"It's Brandon's cat, Hunter. Not yours."

"I know. But *Fluffy?*"

She giggled.

He draped his arm around her shoulders. "You did nice work today, Willingham," he said, gesturing toward the clean driveway with his other hand.

"You didn't do badly yourself, Townsend," she retorted, sliding her arm around his waist.

"And just to show you what a fine gentleman I am," he said as they started walking toward her house, "I'll let you have first dibs on your bathroom."

"Gee! But why are you being so generous?"

"Because I plan on soaking in the tub, and I don't want you complaining that I've used all the hot water."

She pinched his waist. "I knew there was an ulterior motive somewhere."

"I'll start warming the soup while you're taking a bath," he said. "And after I finish mine, we'll have a quick lunch."

"What's the rush?"

"Have you forgotten already? This is the day we get started on our life of crime."

Chapter Eleven

The power came back on while Hunter was taking a bath. Things were gradually returning to normal, Susan thought. Instead of being relieved, she was strangely disappointed, as if a big adventure was coming to an end.

She saw the pan of soup that he had heated and then left on the hearth to keep warm for their lunch. What a dear, thoughtful man he was! With a sigh, she lifted the pan and carried it to the kitchen, where she put it on a burner to continue warming.

Then she went to the telephone and dialed Michael's number. She didn't want to talk to him—she actually dreaded it—but knew she owed it to him.

"Hello, Michael," she said when he answered.

"Susan! I've been trying to reach you all morning."

"We've been outside," she replied, deliberately using the plural pronoun.

"You were playing in the snow?" he asked incredulously.

"Not this time," she said, remembering that she'd told him she might build a snowman. "I shoveled snow while Hunter cut up the tree that fell in my front yard."

"That sounds like quite a bit of work."

"It was. But we cleared the driveway."

"Well, that's good news. Does that mean you'll be able to drive your car again?"

"Yes. I told Hunter that I'd drive him to...uh, an appointment as soon as the roads are clear."

"Good! You'll finally be rid of him," Michael said cheerfully. "I heard on the radio that things are almost back to normal."

Susan remembered thinking the same thing a short while before. The big difference was that she wasn't nearly as happy about it as Michael sounded. "I suppose so."

"Susan," he said, hesitantly this time. "I, uh, know I was a bit dictatorial yesterday."

Dictatorial? She certainly agreed with that, and could add more adjectives to the list of charges against him—high-handed, selfish, arrogant, pompous. They were things she'd never known about him before, and was only glad she'd discovered in time.

"I was presumptuous, too," he said. "Even though we *are* engaged, we're not married yet."

And we never will be. She had decided this morning to call off their engagement. It would be so easy to do right now, but her conscience demanded that she tell him in person.

"That's something we need to talk about, Michael," she said. "But not over the phone."

"I couldn't agree more. Shall I come over to your house tonight?"

"No!" she exclaimed. Until that second, she hadn't thought about where Hunter would be tonight. Quite possibly, he could be here. Even if he wasn't, she knew she'd still feel his presence in the house. This was the place where they'd laughed and fought, survived a storm and shared a bed.

She had no idea where—if anywhere—her relationship with Hunter would lead, and he wasn't the reason she had decided to break off with Michael. Michael was the reason she'd decided to break off with Michael.

"I, uh, I'm not sure how long it'll take me to drive Hunter to his appointment," she said. "I'll get in touch with you later."

"Very well," Michael agreed.

Susan's palms were sweating by the time they said goodbye. She hated half truths and evasions, even if they were sometimes necessary in order to be kind.

HUNTER WATCHED Susan with admiration as she expertly steered the BMW through the slippery, winding hills and valleys of Buckhead. The residential area had been the enclave of Atlanta's "old money" families since the 1920s, and was holding up well, he noticed.

Despite the messy mixture of snow, sand and slush on the public roads, the homes sitting well back from the street seemed untouched by time or nature. They were like pictures from a winter wonderland painted by Norman Rockwell, if he'd chosen to paint millionaires instead of common folk.

Slowing down, Susan made a right turn through an impressive gateway off West Paces Ferry Road. Hunter recognized the entrance to the estate Kenneth Brantley had inherited from his family. He had driven past it many times before, but had never been inside the gates. At the time he and Susan were engaged, Brantley had rented the place to a diplomat from someplace or other.

Hunter gave a long, drawn-out whistle when Susan rounded a curve and he saw the imposing stucco mansion for the first time.

Susan gave him a questioning glance.

"I've never been this close to conspicuous consumption before," he said.

She smiled. "You're just saying that because all this belongs to Kenneth."

"No, I really mean it. Even the maharaja's place was a dump compared to this."

She laughed. "Actually, it could use some work—a lot of work—but Kenneth keeps putting it off until his finances improve."

Hunter frowned as he suddenly remembered being suspicious of some of the bank's loan practices several years ago. After he'd reported his suspicions to his immediate supervisor, he'd been called on the carpet by Brantley himself. At the time, he'd attributed his chastisement to the fact that Brantley didn't like him personally.

Now he wondered if some of those loans had proved as unsound as he'd thought at the time. All told, they were sizable enough to create a serious problem for the bank, and possibly for Brantley's personal finances, as well.

Another thought occurred to him. Susan had told him that her fiancé's family owned a big bank in Switzerland. If Susan actually went through with the marriage to Verner—which Hunter devoutly hoped would never happen—wouldn't a merger between the two families' banks be possible, too? That could solve Brantley's financial problems in a hurry.

"I thought I'd drive around to the back rather than park in front," Susan said, interrupting his thoughts. "Just in case someone drops in unexpectedly."

"That's a good idea," Hunter agreed, his mind still buzzing with possibilities. He waited until she'd parked the car and turned off the engine.

"I was wondering," he began casually. "Has your stepfather known Verner's family for long?"

"What?" she asked swiveling in her seat to look at him.

"You told me that Brantley introduced you to Michael only a short time ago. But I wondered if he'd known the family before then."

"Why do you ask?" she said with a frown.

"Call it curiosity."

"I believe Kenneth has known Michael *and* his family for several years."

Aha! he thought. *The plot thickens.*

"I...I wasn't exactly truthful with you about when I met Michael for the first time," Susan continued.

"What?" Hunter asked, taken by surprise.

"I was angry and I lied to you," she said. "Kenneth did introduce us—like I told you—but it didn't happen a few months ago. It was...almost two years ago."

"You mean it was right after..."

"Yes. Right after you disappeared. I was terribly despondent. Kenneth and Mother thought it would 'cheer me up,' as they called it, if I accompanied them to a bankers' convention in Ponte Vedra. At that point, I didn't much care where I was or what I did, so

I went with them. That's when Kenneth introduced me to Michael.''

Hunter reached over to take her hand, holding it between both of his. ''I suppose this means there was no whirlwind romance, either.''

''Hardly. We saw each other a few times. Then Michael's bank opened an office in Atlanta about nine months ago and we started going out on a regular basis. We became engaged six months ago.''

''Thank you for telling me the truth,'' he said, squeezing her hand before releasing it.

''Now it's your turn to be truthful with me,'' she said. ''What's the real reason you wanted to know how long Kenneth had known the Verners? Was it because you thought he might have prompted the match between Michael and me in order to set up a merger between the two banks, as well?''

Hunter's mouth dropped open. Had she read his mind?

Susan laughed. ''Don't look so shocked. Your thinking was obvious—you brought up the Verners right after I mentioned Kenneth's financial difficulties. Any dummy could figure out what you had in mind.''

''I doubt that,'' he said, trying to sound indignant.

''Besides,'' she added, ''the same thought had occurred to me.''

''It had?''

She nodded. ''But I never allowed Kenneth's ulterior motives and machinations to determine the course of my life. I'm the only one responsible for my decisions.''

''Including your decision to marry Verner?'' Hunter asked, looking her directly in the eyes.

She inhaled sharply, but her gaze didn't waver. "Yes."

"I see." Hunter was the first to look away. He took a deep breath. "Well, I suppose it's time for us to get started."

"Okay." She began to get out of the car but Hunter put his hand out to detain her.

"Wait," he said. "Let's go over our stories one more time to make sure we have them straight."

"Can't we do it on the way?" she asked. "I don't have a key to the back door, so we'll have to walk all the way around to the front."

With a shrug, Hunter released her and opened the car door. He made sure to carry his cane with him.

Susan met him at the back of the car and they started walking. "I forgot to ask Kenneth if the housekeeper would be here today," she said, "but it's supposed to be her day off. If she *is* here, I'll simply tell her the same story we agreed on—that the IRS called me, and I need to look up something in my tax records."

Hunter grunted. "I still think it's strange that you leave your personal tax records at your stepfather's house."

"It's not, really. A man at Kenneth's bank does my taxes, and Mother's taxes, too, so it's convenient to keep all the records together here." She grinned at him. "It's only a lucky coincidence that they're stored in a file cabinet in the same room where Kenneth keeps his health records in a desk."

Hunter sighed. "And my story is that you're driving me to my sister's apartment—heaven forbid!—and decided to stop off here for a few minutes, since it's on the way. I didn't want to wait in a cold car, so I came inside with you."

She nodded, then she frowned. "Do you think our stories are *too* simple?"

"No. If we make them too involved, we might forget what we planned to say."

Susan snickered. "Here we are. Do you think you can manage the steps okay?"

"I'd better hold on to you, to be on the safe side," he said, draping his arms around her shoulder. There were a few advantages to having a sprained ankle, he decided.

The double front doors were massive and made of some exotic wood he couldn't identify. "Nice doors," he commented to Susan as she pressed the doorbell. Chimes echoed from somewhere inside the house.

"Kenneth's ancestors had them imported from some ruined castle in Wales," she said, pressing the bell again.

They waited a while longer, then Susan took out her key and opened the door. Hunter followed her inside and looked around the foyer, which was larger than some houses he'd seen.

"What do you think?" Susan asked, closing the door behind them.

"Shh! I'm still gawking," he said, training his gaze on a winding staircase that looked like something out of a movie.

"Would you like to take a quick tour?" she asked. "Some of the rooms are pretty impressive."

He shook his head. "Thanks, but I'm saving myself for the Taj Mahal. Which way is the room where he keeps the records?"

"Follow me."

He'd half expected Brantley's private study to be on the second floor and was dreading having to negotiate those winding stairs, but Susan led him to a paneled room that opened off the downstairs library instead. "Here we are," she said, shutting the door.

Hunter's heart started beating faster as he walked across the room to a mahogany desk. "Is this it?"

Susan nodded. "The middle drawer on the right."

Hunter sat down in the chair behind the desk. Taking a deep breath, he reached to pull out the drawer. It wouldn't budge. He tried again. "It must be locked," he said, looking at Susan. "Do you know where he keeps the key?"

She frowned. "I didn't even know it had a lock."

Hunter tried the center drawer. It opened easily, but all he saw inside were odds and ends—pens and pencils, paper clips, rubber bands and such. No key.

Susan had walked over to stand beside him. "I suppose we could get a screwdriver or something and pry it open if we have to," she said. "Although I'd rather not do that."

"Me, neither," he said, wondering how much prison time he could get for breaking and entering. He ran his fingers underneath the center drawer, but didn't find anything. Then he saw a small niche between the drawers on the side and the one in the center. He stuck his hand in the niche and felt around.

He grinned when his fingers touched the unmistakable outline of a key. "I think I've found it," he said. He turned the key and pulled on the handle of the second drawer again. It slid open easily.

"Whew!" Susan said.

"I couldn't agree more," Hunter told her. "Now you'll have to show me what we're looking for."

The drawer was deep, and its contents were stored vertically. Susan pulled the drawer all the way open, leafed through several folders, then withdrew a hard-bound record book, approximately twelve by fifteen inches and several inches thick.

"Here you are!" she said triumphantly, plopping the book on the desk in front of him.

Hunter felt as if he'd just been handed the Magna Carta, or something equally consequential. It was a momentous occasion. "Where should I start—front or back?" he asked.

"Just jump in anywhere, I suppose."

He opened the book. "Mmm," he said after a moment.

"What?" Susan asked anxiously.

"Nothing. Just 'Mmm.'"

"You wretch," she said, swatting him lightly on the shoulder.

Hunter flipped through a few pages, scanning the entries quickly. "How many doctors have treated your stepfather in his lifetime?"

"There's no telling how many. Scads."

"He must have spent a fortune on prescriptions alone."

"It's possible."

"Why does he do it? Is he really ill?"

"Oh, no. He says that hypochondria keeps him healthy."

Hunter shook his head and kept flipping pages. Susan leaned over his shoulder to look with him, and put her hand on his other shoulder for balance. He caught a whiff of her perfume and tried not to let himself be too distracted by her close presence.

"There it is!" Susan suddenly cried, pointing her finger at an entry. "Dr. Wayne Estep!"

"Damn!" Hunter said, looking at the entry.

"What?"

"The address listed here is on Peachtree Road, close to Piedmont Hospital."

"So?"

"It's an old address—the one he had when I went to him for my physical. He's not there any longer."

"Darn. But at least he's listed. The entries are in chronological order, so we'll probably find him listed again later in the book."

Hunter sighed and turned another page.

Sometime later—he wasn't sure how long it had been—Hunter heard a noise coming from somewhere inside the house. At the same time, he felt Susan's hand tighten on his shoulder.

"Did you hear that?" she whispered.

Hunter nodded and covered her hand with his while he listened.

"There it is again!" she said after a moment. "I'd better see what it is."

"Not you. Me," he said, getting up from the chair. "I'll see what it is . . . or who."

"Don't play macho with me, Hunter. It's perfectly okay for me to be in Kenneth's house, but you shouldn't be here."

"That may be true, but nobody else is supposed to be here, either."

Her eyes widened. "You mean . . . it might be a burglar?"

"It's possible. So you stay put while I check out the noise."

"No," Susan stated firmly. "We'll both go."

Hunter could see that it was useless arguing with her. "Okay," he said in resignation. "But you stay behind me. Understand?"

She nodded. Hunter picked up his cane and headed for the door. He put his ear against it for a moment, listening, but didn't hear anything. Slowly, he turned the knob and opened the door. He looked into the library and saw it was deserted. The door leading to the hallway was ajar.

"Did we leave that door open?" he whispered to Susan.

She squinched her eyes. "I don't remember."

They made their way across the library. Susan followed so closely behind Hunter that she kept bumping into him. They were almost to the door when Hunter heard another sound—like metal clanging against metal. He stopped in his tracks and Susan bumped against his arm. Hunter dropped his cane, and it made a loud, clattering noise on the parquet floor.

Hunter quickly reached down and retrieved the cane. He held his breath, listening, but the only sound he heard was his own heart thumping against his chest. Susan was right beside him—hanging on to him—and he felt her heart beating a tattoo against his arm.

Susan stiffened at the exact moment he heard another sound—the unmistakable and chilling sound of footsteps. Someone was in the hall...moving slowly, stealthily toward them.

Hunter leaned over to whisper in Susan's ear. "Get behind the door and stay there!" he said urgently. "I mean it!"

She nodded in acquiescence. Hunter shifted his cane—intending to use it as a weapon rather than a crutch, if necessary—and started for the hallway again.

Trying to be as quiet as possible, he silently cursed when his Wellington boots—the only shoes he had that were large enough to fit over the elastic bandage around his ankle—made a slight squeaking sound on the wooden floor. There was nothing he could do about it, though, so he continued onward.

Finally reaching the open doorway, Hunter took one last deep breath, lifted his cane above his head and stepped through it. Then he stopped dead in his tracks.

Standing in the hallway directly in front of him, no more than ten feet away, was a huge mountain of a man. He was well over six feet tall and probably weighed close to three hundred pounds. Dressed like a workman in dark coveralls, the man had a bushy red beard and a wild, menacing look in his eyes.

The thing that caught and held Hunter's attention most, however, was the evil-looking, heavy metal pipe wrench the man wielded in his beefy hand, poised for attack.

The two of them stared at each other, not moving, for what seemed an eternity to Hunter, but probably was only a matter of seconds. The man was the first to move, lifting the wrench fractionally in a threatening gesture as he took a single step forward.

"You better have a good story, mister," he said in a deep, threatening voice.

Hunter blinked, taken aback by the man's words. Who was the intruder here, anyway? He shook his head to clear it, and raised the cane in his own threatening gesture. "This is private property. I'd suggest you get out now, before somebody gets hurt."

"The one getting hurt won't be me," the man said.

Hunter tried another tack. "I'll give you three seconds to leave. Then I'm calling the police."

The man laughed derisively. He took another step. "No, you're not."

"Try me," Hunter challenged, standing his ground.

The man nodded, as if he'd accepted the challenge, and started moving forward again. He held the heavy pipe wrench ready to attack. Hunter knew his cane was no match as a weapon, but he lifted it higher, anyway, preparing for the onslaught. He drew in a deep breath and held it.

"Stop it! Both of you!" Susan yelled, rushing into the hall.

Hunter turned to her. "I told you to stay in the library!" he said angrily. "What the hell are you doing here?"

"What the hell are *you* doing?" she countered. "And you, George," she said to the burly stranger. "Put down that wrench immediately!"

"Ms. Wi-Willingham," the man stammered. "I...I didn't know... Is this fella with you?"

"I'm afraid he is," she replied. "Put down the cane, Hunter."

He did as he was told. "What's going on?"

"This is George Wilson. He occasionally does work for Kenneth," she explained to Hunter before returning her attention to the other man. "Sorry about the confusion, George. We didn't know anyone else was in the house."

"I just let myself in a little while back," George said. "Mr. Brantley asked me to stop by and fix a leak in the downstairs bathroom."

"I'm here to pick up some papers...personal tax records to show the IRS," she said.

George nodded knowingly. "They're all a bunch of busybodies, if you ask me."

"How true," Susan agreed with a smile. "Well, don't let us keep you from your work. We'll let ourselves out as soon as I find what I'm looking for."

"Nice seeing you again, Ms. Willingham," the man said.

"Same here, George," she replied. "Take care."

Hunter waited until they were safely back in Brantley's study, with the door closed behind them, to exhale a tremendous sigh of relief.

"Same here," Susan said, repeating herself.

They continued where they'd left off, looking through Kenneth Brantley's medical records book.

Some time later, Hunter flipped over the last page. "That's it," he said with disgust. "Nothing."

"We must have missed it," Susan said.

"With both of us looking? Not likely. That one old listing for Dr. Wayne Estep is all there is."

"Let's go back again, anyway. Maybe Kenneth listed him differently."

"How? As John Doe?"

"Very funny, Hunter," she said. "Now start looking. Let's begin at the end and work backward this time."

He started turning pages again. "You might have a point, after all," he said. "Look for something unusual...anything."

"Wait!" Susan said a little later. "Go to the page you just passed."

Hunter went back.

"There!" she said triumphantly, pointing to the listing she'd noticed.

"Green Acres Pavilion," Hunter read aloud. Then, "Wow!"

"What?"

"Look at this little notation in parenthesis—W.E.," he said excitedly. "What does that mean to you?"

"Dr. Wayne Estep!" she exclaimed with something close to awe. "We've found him! But there's no address," she added a moment later.

"Green Acres Pavilion sounds sort of like a nursing home," Hunter said.

"I'll get the Yellow Pages," Susan volunteered.

She plopped the thick volume down on the desk a few seconds later. Together, they looked under Nursing Homes, but found no listing for Green Acres.

"I have an idea," Hunter said. He flipped the pages. "Eureka!" he said. "Here it is, listed under Psychologists. What do you know," he said, reading from the display ad. "Green Acres is a residential counseling center for people with mental health problems."

"Do you think Dr. Estep is a patient there?"

"That would be my guess," Hunter said, writing the address and phone number for Green Acres on a notepad.

"Or maybe he's on the staff," Susan said.

"That's a possibility, too." Hunter tore off the note, folded it and put it in the pocket of his jeans. He closed the record book and put it back in place. Then he locked the drawer. "Does everything look the same as it did when we arrived?" he asked Susan.

She nodded. "Are we leaving now?"

"The sooner the better, as far as I'm concerned," he said, getting up from the desk and pulling on his jacket. "Unless you want to hang around and have cocktails and chitchat with your stepfather when he gets home. I'm sure he'd adore seeing me again…and in his own home, too."

Susan made a face at him. Then she led the way out of the bastion of conspicuous consumption. Hunter breathed a sigh of relief when they were finally back in her car and on their way. "I really appreciate all you've done, Susan," he said.

"You're welcome." She hesitated. "That sounded like goodbye."

"Well, I imagine you'll be relieved to have your house to yourself again. And I'm sure Verner will be ecstatic to learn that I've left."

She gave him a strange look before returning her attention to her driving. "What are your plans?" she asked.

"I thought it was obvious. I'm going to rent a car and drive up to Green Acres. I think it's time I paid a little visit to Dr. Wayne Estep." *Two years past time*, he thought.

"That address was in Dahlonega," she said.

"So?"

"It's over an hour's drive from Atlanta. And it's almost five o'clock now. It'll be dark soon."

"I'm a big boy now. It's okay if I stay out after dark."

"There's been a lot of freeway construction since you left, too, all sorts of new twists and turns, exits and entrances."

Hunter looked at her for a long moment. "Is all this leading to something in particular?" he finally asked.

"Yes. I'll drive you up to Dahlonega myself."

He held his breath. Her offer was unexpected. Totally. He thought about mentioning her fiancé's predictable reaction to their driving off together, but didn't because he remembered the strange look she'd given him when he'd mentioned Verner earlier.

"There are no strings... if that's what's taking you so long to make up your mind," she added. "I merely want to see the outcome of all our detective work. I want to hear what Dr. Estep has to say."

"I gratefully accept your offer to drive me to Green Acres," he said formally. "And I didn't take all *that* long to make up my mind."

SUSAN WASN'T surprised that her offer to drive Hunter to Dahlonega had come as a shock to him. She'd been shocked herself when the words came tumbling from her mouth. She certainly hadn't planned them.

Now that she thought about it, she was glad she'd made the offer, and even happier that he'd accepted. It meant that the adventure they'd shared wasn't quite over yet... they had more time to spend together.

Also, she was almost as anxious as Hunter to know what light Dr. Estep could shed on what had happened to him two years ago. She especially wondered what had brought on Hunter's amnesia, the affliction that had come close to destroying her life as well as his. Maybe Dr. Estep could offer the key that would unlock that particular mystery.

Or maybe Dr. Estep was in no condition to offer help to anyone. If that was the case, Hunter would be devastated, and she wanted to be there to help him through his disappointment.

Susan drove by her house before they set out for Dahlonega. While Hunter was loading his belongings—all of them—into her car, Susan packed a small bag for herself, just in case they were detained and had to spend the night. Then she telephoned her mother to let her know where she was going.

"You and Hunter must be hitting if off very well if you're driving him all the way to Dahlonega in this weather," Helen Brantley said.

"I'm simply doing him a favor because he doesn't have a car," Susan lied.

"I'm sure he could afford to rent one," her mother said.

"Besides, it's not that far to drive and the weather's not that bad anymore."

"It's far enough and it's bad enough," her mother said, contradicting both arguments. "But it's not necessary to defend the trip to me. I've always liked Hunter. You know that."

"I know."

"It's the other one that I've never much cared for. But you must know that."

This was the first time Susan had heard that particular news. "Are you talking about Michael?"

"Is there another fiancé you haven't told me about?"

"Mother!" Susan chided.

They both laughed.

"And speaking of that other one," Helen said when she stopped laughing, "how does Michael feel about your feelings toward Hunter, and about the two of you going off together?"

"I don't know," Susan replied seriously. "I haven't told him yet."

"Are you going to tell him?"

"Yes. I plan to stop by his apartment on our way out of town."

"Well! I'd like to be a fly on the wall during *that* conversation!"

"You're impossible, Mother."

"I know. Aren't you glad?"

HUNTER DRUMMED his fingers on his knees while he waited impatiently for Susan to get back to the car. She'd been up in Verner's apartment for a long time now. He looked at his watch again. She'd been gone over half an hour. Damn! What was she doing up there all this time? What were *they* doing?

He had half a mind to get out and call a cab. Susan knew very well that he was anxious to get on the road. He'd hoped to see Dr. Estep today. *Tonight,* he corrected himself.

What *were* they doing up there so long?

He knew what he'd be doing if he was Verner and Susan was *his* fiancée.

They'd better not be doing *that!*

He didn't know why Susan had insisted on stopping by Verner's apartment in the first place. Couldn't she have told him whatever it was she had to say over the phone just as well?

Then he saw her come out of the apartment building and start across the parking lot. She was walking fast, huddling inside her jacket with the collar turned up against the wind. She was hatless, and the wind whipped her long hair around her head. He smiled.

"Sorry it took me so long," Susan said as she slid behind the steering wheel.

"That's okay," Hunter said. "I enjoyed the wait."

She paused before turning the ignition switch and looked at him. "Why?"

"It gave me time to plan what I'm going to say to Dr. Estep."

"Oh." Susan started the car and pulled out of the parking space.

It wasn't until she turned the BMW onto Peachtree Road that Hunter noticed her hands on the steering wheel, illuminated by the glare of a streetlight.

He blinked. Twice.

He stopped breathing.

His heart skipped a beat.

The engagement ring Verner had given her was a huge showy diamond—way too large for her delicate fingers. She'd been wearing the ring when she went upstairs to see him.

She wasn't wearing it now.

Her ring finger was bare.

Chapter Twelve

"The roads are getting worse," Susan commented.

"No kidding." For the past half hour, Hunter had been riding with one eye closed and both fists clenched as the BMW skidded first one way, then the other. If Susan weren't such a good driver, they'd have wound up in a ditch—or worse—long before now.

"They must have received a lot more snow up here than we did in Atlanta," she said.

"It sure looks like it," he agreed. The farther north they went, the more treacherous driving conditions were. Even the roads that had been partially cleared during the day had started to ice over again now that the sun was down and the temperature had dropped.

"Those icy black patches are the worst," Susan said. "You can't even see them. You just know you've hit one when you start to sli—"

They started sliding before she finished the sentence. Hunter held on for dear life while the car went sideways down the highway for a number of yards before Susan was able to correct their course.

"I see what you mean," Hunter said when he caught his breath once more. He glanced at Susan and saw her hands clenched around the steering wheel. "Are you okay?"

"A little shaken," she replied. "But otherwise..." She hesitated. "Only fair," she admitted.

"I'd offer to drive if it weren't for my bad ankle."

"Thanks, anyway. Besides, I'm more familiar with the car than you are."

"Maybe we should stop for the night at a motel," he suggested. He was anxious to see the doctor, but stopping seemed a good idea under the circumstances. "We can get a fresh start tomorrow."

"I've been thinking the same thing. Except I haven't seen a motel in ages. Have you?"

"No," he admitted. "But I'll start looking harder."

They drove along in silence. Once or twice, Hunter saw Susan lift her hand to rub the back of her neck. *Tension,* he thought.

"At least there's not much traffic," she said.

That could be either a blessing or a curse, he reckoned. If they slid off the road, it could be a long time before someone came by to help them.

"Would you like to pull onto the shoulder and rest?" he asked.

"I've considered doing just that," she said. "But it's too dangerous. Someone could come along and ram into us."

Hunter tried to think of some way to help her, but came up empty. He concentrated on watching out for a motel. "We should be close to Dahlonega," he said, seeing the headlights of a car approaching from the opposite direction.

Susan nodded. "I think it's only a few miles."

Hunter squinted. Wasn't that car coming toward them faster than it should under these dangerous conditions? "Susan," he said. "That car..."

"I see it," she said. "The driver is going way too fast. I'll slow down."

Hunter kept track of the approaching vehicle's breakneck speed. Then, as he watched helplessly, the other car started skidding. In a flash, it was in their lane, spinning around and around as it hurtled toward them.

"Susan!" he yelled. "My God!"

She had no choice but to hit the brakes—hard—and try to swerve out of the way of the oncoming car. Hunter felt a jolt and heard the sound of metal on metal as some part of the BMW collided with the other vehicle. Then he felt a second jolt as they started spinning, too.

Tires screeched and Susan screamed. He reached out blindly, but couldn't find her. He felt a third jolt—much stronger this time, strong enough to throw him forward, then back against the seat. After that, there was silence.

"Hunter!"

A hand shook his shoulder, and he opened his eyes. Susan was leaning across the console, her face close to his. "Are you all right?" she asked anxiously.

He nodded. "Just...had the breath...knocked out of me."

"That damned driver!" she said. "He could have killed us."

He touched Susan's cheek with his fingers. "That was some fine driving you did, Ms. Willingham. You probably saved both our skins. Are you okay?"

"I'm fine. Just mad as hell."

"What happened to the other car?" Hunter asked.

She shook her head. "I don't know. I'm not even sure I know what happened to us. I *think* we're in a ditch."

"I'd better get out and take a look," he said, unsnapping his seat belt.

"Not without me, you're not." She unsnapped her own belt, then leaned across him to open the glove compartment. "I'll bring a flashlight."

Hunter opened his door and stepped into snow several inches deep. "Be careful when you get out," he cautioned Susan. "The car's all the way off the shoulder and resting on a fairly steep incline."

He closed the door, but held on to the BMW, feeling his way gingerly. Susan had left the headlights on, but the front of the vehicle was angled upward, so they didn't do a whole lot of good. He felt rather than saw the dent in the rear fender.

"There's a big dent in the left rear fender," Susan called from the other side of the car.

"There's one on this side, too," Hunter said. He moved around to the back. "The bumper seems to be okay."

As his eyes adjusted to the darkness, Hunter saw that the incline wasn't nearly as steep as he'd thought when he first stepped out of the car. In fact, with him pushing and Susan at the wheel, they just might be able to get it back on the road by themselves.

Then he took a step and the pain he felt reminded him of his sprained ankle. To hell with it! He wouldn't let a little sprain prevent them from getting the car moving again...not if the alternative was spending the night trying to keep from freezing to death out here in the middle of nowhere.

"I don't understand how both rear fenders were hit, and neither of these were," Susan said when he joined her at the front of the car.

"Well, you swerved in time to avoid a head-on collision but not in time to keep the other car from hitting your rear end."

"That explains the dent on the driver's side," she said. "But what about the other side?"

Hunter shook his head. "Beats me."

"Shouldn't we go up to the road and see what happened to the other car?" Susan asked.

"I'll go. You stay here."

"No. I'm going with you."

"Susan, there's no telling what we'll find."

"I'm still going."

"Stubborn woman," he muttered, starting toward the road.

"You're pretty stubborn yourself," she said, moving to his side.

"What makes you say that?"

"Otherwise, you'd have your arm around my shoulders to take some weight off that bad ankle."

Hunter grunted. Then he draped his arm around her shoulders.

When they reached the highway, they saw no trace of the other car, only tire tracks. "Let's walk back the way we came," Hunter said. "He could have spun off the road, too."

Several yards down the road, they came to a guardrail. "Here's what caused the dent in your right fender," he said. "The impact of the blow from the other car sent the BMW into a spin, and we must have hit the guardrail. I remember feeling a second jolt."

"So do I, now that you mention it. At the time, I was too busy to notice much of anything."

Aiming the flashlight at the railing, they walked along its length. "Here's where we must have hit," Susan said, touching her hand to a spot. "There's red paint."

"That's it," Hunter agreed. "Let me have the light for a second, will you?" Susan handed it to him and he aimed it over the railing while they both looked.

Susan inhaled sharply. Hunter felt slightly ill. "That's where we would have landed if it hadn't been for the guardrail," he said, staring at the deep ravine. "It saved our lives."

They continued staring silently until Hunter squeezed Susan's shoulder. "We were so lucky," she said softly.

"Yes." He gave her another squeeze. "Let's walk a little farther. If we don't find the other car by then, it means the driver probably regained control and drove away."

"You mean he simply left us, just like that?" Susan said incredulously.

"Any driver who would drive the way that one did is capable of anything," Hunter stated.

They searched both sides of the highway, but found no trace of the vehicle that had forced them off the road. No other cars had come by, either, Hunter noticed as they made their way back to Susan's BMW. He mentioned it to her.

"It's not a good sign," he said. "It means it's up to us to get your car back on the road."

"Can we do it by ourselves?"

"Sure," he said, trying to sound confident. "You drive and I'll push. We shouldn't have too much of a problem."

"What about your sprained ankle?"

"I'll put all the pressure on my other ankle. Don't worry."

When they reached her car, Hunter walked all around it again, inspecting the terrain and the position of each tire.

"Your front wheels are aimed straight ahead. That's good," he told Susan. "The bad thing is, once you reach the highway, you'll be headed the wrong way. But don't worry about it. There's no traffic, and it'll be easy enough to turn around."

Hunter decided to have Susan get in the car and try to drive it out of the ditch on its own one time, just in case, by some miracle, it was able to make it.

It wasn't.

The wheels spun futilely in the snow without gaining traction. "Okay, that's enough," he called to her. "Kill the engine and let's go to plan two."

At Hunter's direction, they started searching for loose gravel, small twigs, anything they could put under the tires that would help get the car moving. They found almost nothing.

"If anything's here, it's hidden by the snow," Susan said with disgust.

Hunter nodded his agreement while he thought. "My belongings!" he said. "I'm sure we can find something in my bags that we can use."

Susan held the flashlight while he hauled out a duffel and started rummaging through it. He pulled out two towels, an undershirt and a terry-cloth robe.

"These should do the trick," he said. "We'll need to dig away the snow in front of each tire and jam these things up underneath."

Susan worked at the front of the car while he concentrated on the rear. He shoveled away snow with his gloved hands until they were numb with cold. He took off his gloves and blew on his fingers to warm them. Then he shoveled some more. Finally, he placed a towel in front of one wheel and the robe in front of the other, pushing them up under the tires as far as he could.

Getting to his feet, he walked to the front of the car to see how Susan was doing. She had finished and was brushing snow from her jean-clad knees.

"You okay?" he asked.

"Except for feeling like a frozen daiquiri, I'm fine," she replied. "Do you think this will work?"

He took her cold hands in his and started massaging them, even though his own hands were equally cold. "I hope so," he said. Then, seeing her crestfallen look, he quickly added, "I'm sure it will."

"It better. I don't relish spending the night stuck in this deep freeze."

"I don't know," he said, trying to tease her out of her glumness. He brought one of her hands to his lips and kissed it. "The whole thing seems a bit romantic to me." He kissed her other hand. "We could even keep each other warm the way we did last night."

"No gentleman would bring that up."

"True. Aren't you glad I'm no gentleman."

"I think," she said, taking a deep breath and gently tugging her hands from his loose grasp, "it's time we made our move."

"I thought that's what I was doing."

"Our move to get out of the ditch."

"Oh. *That* move," he said with an exaggerated sigh. "If you insist . . ."

Hunter waited beside the car while Susan climbed inside and started the engine. She lowered the driver-side window.

"I'll start pushing the car at the count of three," he said. "Just remember to accelerate gradually. And once you feel the car start moving, don't stop until you reach the highway. Okay?"

She nodded.

Hunter made his way to the rear of the car. When he leaned over to position his shoulder against the trunk, he felt a sharp pain in his ankle. He tried to ignore it, pretending the pain belonged to someone else, not him.

"Ready?" he yelled to Susan.

"Ready!" she yelled back.

"Okay. One . . . two . . . *three!*"

He gave a mighty push—as hard as he could. An involuntary groan escaped his lips as searing pain shot through his ankle. The BMW's wheels were spinning madly, shooting a steady stream of snow into his face.

He kept pushing . . . harder . . . harder . . .

Suddenly, the car lurched and moved forward, gaining momentum as it went . . . and causing Hunter to lose his balance and fall flat on his face in the snow. He laughed and kept on laughing—like a crazy man— as the car sped away.

By damn, they'd done it!

He was still chuckling as he got to his feet. He brushed away snow from his face and clothes, then hobbled toward the highway.

By the time he got there, Susan had already turned the vehicle around and was waiting for him.

"Where to, mister?" she asked when he opened the door. "You look like you could use a lift."

"I sure could, especially if we're talking about more than a ride in a car."

"That's all we're offering at these rates. Take it or leave it."

"In that case . . ." He got in the car.

"I'll tell you the truth, Hunter," Susan said, starting the BMW in motion again. "I'm relieved that we escaped that mess with only damage to the car and not to us."

"We were lucky," he agreed.

"How's your ankle?"

"It's fine," he said, ignoring the throbbing pain. "It'll be even better when I can soak it, along with the rest of my body, in a tub of hot water."

"Don't talk about it!" she said. "Just keep looking for a motel."

Several miles down the road, they finally spotted one. Susan slowed to a crawl. Even so, the car skidded as they pulled into the parking lot. Connally's Motel was a one-story concrete-block structure consisting of no more than ten or twelve units, most of them with pickup trucks parked in front.

"What do you think?" she asked uncertainly.

"Well, it's not the Ritz, but on the other hand it's not deserted," he said cautiously. "I guess that's a good sign."

"And we haven't seen anything else," she added.

"That's true. There might not even be any rooms available here."

"Let's at least go into the office and talk to the desk clerk," she said decisively.

"Right."

The motel office was small, brightly lit and furnished entirely in knotty pine Early American. A middle-aged balding man in glasses sat on a stool behind the counter reading a magazine. He looked up with surprise when they entered.

"Good evening," Hunter said.

The man nodded. "Terrible night to be out."

"That's for sure," Hunter agreed.

"My name's Connally," the man said, extending his hand across the counter. "Lester Connally."

"As in Connally's Motel?" Hunter asked with a smile as they shook hands.

"That's right. I bought the place when I retired from Georgia Power. About five years it's been now."

"My name's Hunter Townsend. Pleased to meet you."

Mr. Connally grinned. "You'll be even more pleased when I tell you I can let you have a room—the last one in the place."

Hunter frowned. He'd assumed he and Susan would each have a private room, and was sure she had assumed the same thing. They hadn't discussed what they would do if only one room was available.

"That *is* why you're here, isn't it—to rent a room?" Mr. Connally asked when Hunter didn't say anything.

Susan suddenly stepped forward. "It certainly is, Mr. Connally. And we'll take the room, won't we, honey?" she said, looping her arm through Hunter's.

"Yes, we will," Hunter said as soon as he recovered from the shock of hearing her address him as "honey." He patted her arm and looked at the motel owner. "This is the little woman, Mr. Connally. My better half."

Susan pinched him so hard, he almost cried out with pain.

Hunter signed the register. "I'm not sure what time we'll be leaving tomorrow," he said. "It might be early. Would you like me to pay in advance?"

Mr. Connally chuckled. "Not unless 'early' means before 5:00 a.m. That's the time I get up. It's a carry-over from my Georgia Power days when we had to get crews on the road at the crack of dawn."

Hunter smiled. "I seriously doubt we'll be up at five."

"My wife puts out a fresh pot of coffee here in the office at about six. Stop by and have some."

"Thank you. That sounds great," Susan said.

The talk about coffee reminded Hunter that the only thing he and Susan had eaten the entire day was soup in the early afternoon. He was suddenly ravenous.

"Is there a restaurant around here still open to-night?" he asked.

"I doubt it, what with the bad weather and all," Mr. Connally said, rubbing the bald spot on his head. "You might try calling the pizza delivery place. The number's listed beside the phone in your room. If they're not open, you're out of luck until morning."

Hunter hurried Susan out of the motel office. He made equally quick work of unpacking the car, even with his bad ankle. Then he picked up the telephone in their room and dialed the number for pizza delivery, sighing with relief when someone answered. He ordered a giant pizza with everything.

SUSAN WAS NERVOUS. She didn't know what to do with herself while she waited for Hunter. She rubbed her wet hair vigorously with a towel, then wound the towel around her head and sat on the side of one of the two double beds. Almost immediately, she jumped up again, unwound the towel and started brushing her hair. After only a few strokes, she put the brush back on the dresser.

She glanced at the door to the bathroom, where Hunter was presumably soaking in a tub of hot water, then looked at her watch. He'd been in there for what seemed like ages but had only been a matter of minutes.

The deliveryman had come and gone during that time, and the pizza he'd ordered was growing cold while it sat untouched in a box on the dresser. She thought about eating a slice, but really wasn't hungry.

She thought about taking off her robe and climbing between the sheets of one of the two beds, but wouldn't that give Hunter the impression she was being extremely forward? Wouldn't he think she was inviting him to join her?

Besides, she wasn't sleepy. Just tired. And antsy. Especially that.

She wished he hadn't insisted that she take a bath first. By all rights, he should have gone first. His clothes were wetter, and there was his sprained ankle in addition to that. But no. He wouldn't hear of it. She'd argued with him for a while, then had given in just to shut him up.

She smiled. He could be stubborn, all right. Headstrong, too. And argumentative. He was also the bravest person she'd ever known. The most thought-ful. The dearest.

He was the man she loved.

She'd loved him for years, and would love him for the rest of her life.

She'd admitted all that to Michael this afternoon when she broke their engagement. It hadn't been a pretty scene. Michael had been bitter, angry—and she couldn't blame him. But as she'd pointed out to him, it would have been worse if she'd gone ahead and married him, knowing she was in love with someone else.

He deserved more than that, she'd told him, some-one who loved him and him alone. She didn't tell him that that someone needed to be more generous and forgiving than she was.

Almost as an afterthought, she'd suggested that Michael might want to talk with a counselor, some-one like Nancy Wages, perhaps. She was kind, under-standing, a good listener. Michael had agreed to see her.

So that was that.

Now what, Susan? she asked herself.

"Good question," she answered out loud.

She walked over to one of the beds and pulled back the covers. Then she took off her robe and got into bed to wait for Hunter to come out of the bathroom.

HUNTER DUCKED his head under the hot water streaming from the shower, not that he had much hope it would clear his thoughts. He'd already soaked in the tub for almost half an hour, and that hadn't helped him make sense of things.

His life was a tangled mess.

He'd finally admitted to himself that he was in love with Susan. He loved her with a passion that hadn't died in two long years, despite what he thought she and/or her stepfather might or might not have done to him.

Judging by appearances, she might be falling in love with him again, too. At least *something* was going on. She was no longer wearing the ring Verner had given her, and had probably broken their engagement.

So...with him loving her and her maybe loving him, too, life should have been wonderful, marvelous, all hearts-and-flowers and happy-ever-afters. It wasn't. And it was his own damned fault.

He'd led her to believe that he'd left her standing at the altar because he'd had amnesia. He could well imagine her total disgust and absolute fury when she found out that it was a lie.

Never mind that it was Susan's mother who'd come up with the idea in the first place. He'd gone along with it. And now his lie had come back to haunt him.

He couldn't suddenly waltz in and tell her he'd been mistaken—that it was a brain tumor instead of amnesia that had caused him to leave her...and that he really hadn't had a brain tumor, either.

"What is this?" she would scoff. "Musical diseases? The disease of the week?"

There was no way on earth that Susan would believe his story about the brain tumor, especially since he had no way of proving it.

His only chance—his only hope—was in the less-than-capable hands of Dr. Wayne Estep. If the doctor remembered him...and remembered telling him he had only a year to live...and would *admit* his error...

Those were a lot of ifs.

Hunter turned off the water and got out of the shower. He could picture Susan in the bedroom, clean and fresh from her bath, warm and sexy, the most desirable woman in the world to him. He wanted to go in there and take her in his arms, hold and kiss her, make mad passionate love to her.

But he couldn't...not while she still believed his lie about having had amnesia. If they made love now, it would only make things worse when she found out the truth. She would feel—and rightly so—that he'd taken advantage of her.

Maybe tomorrow, things would be different. Dr. Estep could solve all his problems...if Hunter was very, very lucky.

He toweled himself dry, pulled on a fresh pair of chinos and a T-shirt and hobbled into the bedroom barefoot. He stopped dead still in his tracks when he saw Susan.

She was in bed.

That in itself was a surprise, because he'd expected her to be up eating pizza or watching TV or something. Anything. But even more surprising was the *way* she was in bed—wide-awake and alert, her green eyes watching him with a look he couldn't decipher, and with the covers pulled up over her shoulders to her neck.

The first thing that struck him was that she might have the covers pulled up because she wasn't wearing any nightclothes. He immediately dismissed that idea as wishful thinking, every guy's fantasy. But still...

"What's wrong?" she asked.

Hunter realized he'd been staring. "Oh. I, uh, was just surprised to see you in bed."

"Why?"

He couldn't come up with a good reason—not one he could tell her—so he shrugged. "Did the pizza come?"

"It's over there on the dresser."

Wouldn't most people have brought their arms out from under the covers and pointed to the pizza? he wondered. *Was* she naked?

He walked over to the dresser. "Would you like me to bring you a piece?"

"No, thanks."

He lifted the lid of the pizza box. "Are you sure? It smells delicious."

"I'm really not hungry."

Suddenly, Hunter realized he wasn't hungry any longer, either. He lowered the lid.

"Aren't you going to eat?" Susan asked.

"In a minute." He hobbled over to stand next to her bed. After a moment's hesitation, he sat down beside her. "Is something wrong?" he asked.

"Why do you say that?"

"You've eaten almost nothing today. And you're in bed."

"I'm tired," she said, as if that answered everything.

She didn't look tired. In fact, her eyes were unusually bright. He touched his palm to her forehead. "You don't have a fever."

She brought her hand outside the covers to push his away impatiently. "I said I was tired, Hunter, not ill."

She had on a nightgown, after all. He felt a perverse disappointment. Then he noticed that the nightgown wasn't her usual Laura Ashley paisley cover-up-everything-in-sight model. It was frilly and gauzy, almost transparent.

He also noticed that the hand she'd used to push his away was her left hand. Her *naked* left hand. He knew he shouldn't do it, but couldn't stop himself. He caught her hand in his and touched her ring finger.

"Do you want to tell me about this?" he asked.

She hesitated a moment. "I broke the engagement."

"Was it...I mean..." He stopped, then started over. "There's not a good way to say what I want to say. Anything will sound egotistical and self-centered but... Did your decision have anything to do with me?"

"Yes," she replied. "And no."

He raised an eyebrow.

"Yes in the sense that seeing you again caused me to take a closer look at myself," she explained. "I re-examined what I thought I wanted out of life, and found out that it wasn't Michael."

"So, in a way, I *am* responsible."

"No, Hunter. Even if you didn't exist, I still wouldn't marry Michael. You don't have to feel responsible or...or obligated."

"You misunderstand what I said!" he exclaimed. "I *want* to be the one responsible for saving you from Verner! I'll always consider that to be one of my major accomplishments in life."

Susan laughed.

Hearing her laugh, Hunter relaxed.

Then she did something that caused him to grow tense again, but in a good way this time. She reached up and put her arms around his neck. He liked the way they felt—as if they belonged there.

"In that case," she said, "I suppose a proper show of gratitude is in order."

"It wouldn't be amiss," he said by way of encouragement.

She pulled his head down and kissed him lightly on the lips. "Thank you," she said.

He shook his head. "It was a major, *major* accomplishment. Surely I deserve more gratitude than that little kiss."

"If you insist," she said, pulling his head down again, slowly.

Their lips met. Hers were soft and warm, sweetly responsive. And when Hunter increased the pressure of his mouth on hers, she parted her lips willingly, allowing his tongue free access.

What had started as a game was turning into something more involved, but that was okay. Kissing was allowed—even encouraged—in the ground rules he'd set for himself.

He closed his eyes and surrendered to the profound pleasure of kissing Susan the way she was meant to be kissed—thoroughly, deeply and with feeling—taking all the time in the world to do it. Something as precious as this shouldn't be rushed.

He couldn't have asked for a more cooperative partner. Susan was with him all the way, meeting him mouth to mouth, tongue to tongue, kiss for kiss. It was as if, suddenly set loose from her entanglement with Verner, she was finally able to enjoy her newfound freedom.

Sometime later—Hunter had no idea how long it had been—he became aware of how much they'd shifted and changed positions since they'd first started kissing. The bed covers were no longer pulled up to

Susan's neck. Somebody had pushed them completely aside. The only things covering Susan now were her frilly, gauzy nightie...and himself.

He was no longer sitting on the bed with his feet on the floor. He was lying beside her, partially on top of her, his arms wrapped as securely around her as hers were around him, their legs intertwined.

And his arousal was significant enough for the whole world to notice. Certainly Susan must have noticed it by now.

He hadn't intended things to go this far...well, maybe *this* far, but certainly no further. He absolutely would not make love to her, even if his entire body was crying out for it to happen.

If he gave in to his desperate need, he'd hate himself in the morning.

And she'd hate him even more when she found out about his lies.

Using all his willpower, Hunter disengaged Susan's arms from around his neck and tore his mouth away from hers. He propped himself up on his elbows.

She opened her eyes and looked at him with confusion. "What?" she asked simply.

"I, uh, that is... We need to slow things down."

"Why?" She reached up to trace his lips with her finger, sending a hot shiver up his spine.

He tried to think of something. Anything. "You're tired."

"I'm not that tired," she said, giving him a seductive smile as she continued teasing him with her finger.

Heaven help me, he thought. "And...and the pizza's getting cold," he stammered, clutching at any straw.

"Pizza! You're thinking about pizza?" she said, withdrawing her finger and her hand along with it.

She sounded incredulous, and he didn't blame her. "Well..."

"Okay," she said, folding her arms across her chest. "Go ahead and eat your pizza. Don't let me stop you."

"Susan..."

She turned her head, refusing to look at him. "Leave me alone."

"Please don't be angry."

"I'm not angry."

"You could have fooled me."

"I'm *not*. I'm...I'm frustrated. And hurt."

"Hurt?" he repeated.

She turned back to him. Her green eyes were flashing. "Why don't you tell the truth, Hunter?"

"What are you talking about?"

"Why don't you just come out and admit that you don't want me...*that* way."

"Not want you!" he exclaimed. "Oh, God! Not want you?"

Feeling as if a dam had burst inside him, Hunter gathered Susan in his arms, ignoring her protests, ignoring her arms that tried to push him away. He started kissing her, all of her—her lips, her cheeks, her neck, her breasts, her nose, her eyebrows, every place he could reach.

He caught her hand in his and brought it to his groin. "Not want you?" he murmured against her neck. "I've wanted you forever. As long as I can remember. A lifetime."

Framing her face with his hands, he gazed into her eyes, then lowered his head until their mouths met. "I'm lost," he whispered against her lips.

SUSAN HEARD Hunter's words—something about being lost—but had no idea what he was talking about. At the moment, she couldn't think rationally. She was drowning in a sea of sensuous pleasure.

Hunter pushed the straps of her nightgown aside and kissed her breasts again, teasing the nipples with a tongue made warm and wet from their kisses. She didn't try to hold back the low moans that escaped her throat.

She moved her hands to his back, letting them roam at will, savoring the sexy warmth of him. She felt the hard male muscles under his T-shirt, and delighted in the solid strength of him.

His mouth returned to her lips, hot and demanding. She was eager to give him all he demanded, and even more than that. She was acutely disappointed when he suddenly pulled away from her.

"You have on too many clothes," he said huskily.

She relaxed and helped him remove her wisp of a nightie. "So do you," she said, her voice equally husky.

He grinned and held up his arms for her to remove his T-shirt. When it was gone, she buried her hands in the crisp, dark hair on his chest. It was much thicker than it had been two years ago, she thought briefly.

His trousers were discarded next. Her eyes widened when she saw he was completely nude underneath.

"I didn't bother putting on undershorts when I got out of the shower," he explained.

"That wasn't what I was thinking about," she said a little breathlessly, keeping her eyes trained on his impressive anatomy.

His chuckle was a low, male rumble that came from deep in his chest. "See anything you like?"

"Oh, yes," she replied. "A lot. A huge amount."

He laughed again. "Now it's your turn."

"What?"

"Your panties. Stop gawking and lie down so I can take them off."

Susan lay back on the bed and arched her hips while Hunter removed her panties and cast them aside. She watched him lean back on his knees to look at her. She kept watching as she saw his gaze roam over her naked body. Desire showed in the dark depths of his eyes—so much so that she no longer doubted that he wanted her.

She wanted him, too, with a headlong fierceness that surprised her. But who wouldn't want him? He was so beautiful!

Then his lips were on hers again, and there was no more time for thought. His hard, bare chest pressed against the softness of her breasts. He moved back and forth across her, eliciting an instantaneous erotic response. His hands, sometimes feather-soft, sometimes boldly aggressive, roamed over her entire body. The hands tickled and teased, delighted and demanded.

With something akin to desperation, she reached out to touch him, too. He was thick and hard and fully aroused. Her throat constricted as she stroked his silky flesh, and a moan escaped her lips.

He pulled back to gaze at her, his dark eyes even darker with desire. She wanted him so much she ached. They looked into each other's eyes, acknowledging the special importance of the moment. They'd known each other before, loved each other before.

But not like this, Susan thought. Not only her body wanted Hunter. Her heart and soul wanted him, too.

He gave a low groan as he lowered himself and entered her—not all at once, but slowly, inch by inch, his body becoming lost inside her body, him becoming lost in her.

This was right, so right, Susan thought as she strained toward him. After two long, lonely years, this was meant to be. She tightened her arms around his neck and wrapped her legs around his hips as he began moving inside her.

She wanted to please him as he pleased her—not only at the moment, in this most intimate way, but in so many other ways, as well. She wanted to make it up to him for those two years they'd spent apart. She turned her head to capture his lips with hers, wanting to love him with every part of her body.

As Hunter made love with her, Susan felt the whole world vibrating with the echo of that love. The echo grew louder, keeping pace with the thundering beat of her heart. She arched her back, reaching . . . reaching for the heavens, for the stars . . .

And then it happened. The moon, the stars, Jupiter, Mars . . . the entire universe came together in one huge, beautiful, wonderful cosmic explosion.

Chapter Thirteen

Hunter held Susan close, listening to the sound of her rapid breathing and to his own, waiting for his hammering heart to slow down. Neither of them spoke, and he was grateful for the silence.

What could he say to her? That he was a liar and a cheat? That he'd never lost his memory, and had lied to her time and again by claiming he had? That he'd violated the one solitary rule he'd set for himself by making love to her when he swore he wouldn't?

He felt awful.

Even worse, and in spite of his terrible guilt, he still savored the euphoria of what had been the most incredible experience of his life—making love with Susan after what seemed like a lifetime of longing.

For two years, he'd carried around the dream of someday holding her in his arms again. He'd denied it, especially to himself, but it had been there all along. The reality was even better than the dream. She'd given herself to him freely, completely, with an unbridled passion that matched his own.

He might hate himself—and he did—but he doubted that he'd change things, even if he could.

He tightened his arms around her, remembering the way she'd responded to him. He remembered the little sounds of pleasure she'd made, and the way she'd cried out during those final, frenzied moments.

Her breathing had slowed now, and her eyelids were closed. He wondered if she'd fallen asleep. After the long, harrowing day they'd had, it was entirely possible. He smiled, recalling the way she had shoveled the driveway this morning...the way she'd intervened to stop what could have been a serious encounter between him and the handyman he'd thought was an intruder at Kenneth Brantley's house.

He recalled her skill while driving over icy, slippery roads, and her courage in the face of potential disaster when that car had come hurtling toward them. And during it all, she had never complained.

Tenderly, he touched his lips to her forehead. She opened her eyes.

"I didn't mean to wake you," he said.

"I wasn't asleep. I was thinking."

"Pleasant thoughts, I hope."

"Very nice," she said, kissing his neck.

"Good." He kissed her cheek.

"There was one thing I wondered about, though."

"What is it?"

"It was something you said just before we made love—something about being lost."

"Oh."

"Do you remember?"

"Yes." He didn't want to lie to her anymore, not unless he had to. "While I was in the bathroom...thinking about you...I made a promise to myself that I wouldn't try to make love with you tonight."

"So I was right about that," she said. "You didn't—"

"It wasn't that I didn't want to. You must know that by now. It was... I knew you'd just broken up with Verner. You were vulnerable. I didn't want to take advantage of you."

"Even if I wanted to be taken advantage of?"

"Especially if you wanted it. I knew you weren't thinking clearly, that you might later regret that we'd made love, and hate me for it." He sighed. "So I made a promise to myself, and then didn't have the willpower to stick to it. I was talking to myself when I said I was lost."

What he'd told her was the truth. But it wasn't all of the truth and he still felt rotten. There was so much he was holding back because he was afraid of her reaction.

"Did you really think I might regret making love with you, Hunter?"

"Yes."

"It's later now," she told him. "And I don't regret that we made love. Not one iota."

"Give it time. The night's not over yet."

"Funny you should mention that. It's the same thing I was thinking."

"That the night's not over yet?" Hunter asked, seeing the mischievous sparkle in her green eyes.

"Exactly. And you know the old saying about in for a penny, in for a pound..." She lifted her hand and started making circles around his tight nipple.

Hunter shivered with pleasure and then grinned. "Are you suggesting that since I'm feeling guilty as sin, anyway..." He kissed her rosy-tipped breast. "We might as well make love again?" He kissed the other breast.

"Absolutely." She blew into his ear. "Let's do something we can both really regret later."

Hunter hauled her into his arms and started putting some serious effort into creating guilt.

SUSAN OPENED her eyes to unfamiliar surroundings. It took her a moment to figure out where she was. Remembering, she felt a warm flood of desire rush through her. Remembering even more, she turned her head to look at Hunter.

He wasn't there.

She picked up her watch from the bedside table and saw that it was almost eight o'clock. Mr. Connally had told them last night that his wife always brought out a fresh pot of coffee in the morning. She hoped that's where Hunter had gone, and that he would bring her a cup, too.

She yawned and stretched, feeling deliciously decadent as she leaned back into the softness of the bed. Then she smiled as she recalled the use she and Hunter had made of it last night. She let her mind wander from generalities to specifics—Hunter's lips on hers, fierce and demanding, his touch on her breasts, between her thighs...

Just thinking of him made her want him all over again. With a little encouragement, she could probably become a dedicated nymphomaniac.

But only with Hunter.

He was the only man who'd ever made her feel this way. He was the only man she'd ever loved this way.

Love. Hunter hadn't mentioned that word to her last night. Not once. He'd whispered words of endearment, words of passion. He'd talked of want and need. Of longing. But not love.

It wasn't important, she told herself. He was probably preoccupied with thoughts of his meeting with Dr. Estep today.

And speaking of Dr. Estep... It was time for her to get out of bed and get herself ready to meet that gentleman. Hunter would probably be in a hurry to get on the road when he returned. Throwing back the covers, she slid out of bed and padded to the bathroom.

A short while later, enjoying the hot stream of water beating down on her skin, she thought she heard a noise from the bedroom. She ducked her head from behind the shower curtain and listened, but didn't hear anything. "Hunter," she called.

There was no answer.

She called again. "Hunter! Is that you?"

"No!" he called back. "It's a Teenage Mutant Ninja Turtle."

Susan turned off the water and stepped out of the shower. "Good," she said, reaching for a towel. "I've been expecting you."

"I brought you coffee," he called. "But if you're not out of the bathroom in five seconds, I'll drink it myself."

She dropped the towel, flung open the door and stepped into the bedroom. She was completely naked and was dripping water onto the carpet. "You'll what?"

His eyes widened, and Susan felt a rush of pleasure when she saw the sudden spark of desire that leaped into them. "You'll what?" she asked again.

She saw a blur of movement, then he was holding her in his arms, lifting her off the floor and gazing into her face. His eyes were so dark, so intense, they made her heart race. "You'll what?" she whispered, looping her arms around his neck.

"I forget," he said, lowering her along his body until his lips captured hers.

"Mmm," she murmured as he started moving them slowly toward the bed, which was in wild disarray from their lovemaking of the night before. She held on tightly, her lips clinging to his, while he lowered her until she felt the bed beneath her back.

He pressed against her and she felt the hardness of him—physical evidence of the need she'd aroused in him. His arousal immediately fired a corresponding need in her. She wanted him with a fierce, primal passion she'd never known before. She wanted him here, now, wanted him inside her, filling her, fulfilling her.

She tore her lips away from his, but only long enough to whisper, "Hurry!"

Hunter was equally urgent. He tore at the snap to his jeans and, fumbling, finally managed to unzip them. He didn't take time to pull them off. He pushed them down instead, along with his undershorts, and plunged himself deep inside her.

She cried out with pleasure. So did he. There was no hesitation. They took each other quickly, roughly, almost desperately in their haste to reach that pinnacle of completion.

She reached it first, but her cries sent him over the edge almost immediately. One more shattering tremor vibrated through his body, and then he collapsed beside her, both of them panting, both their bodies covered with a sheen of perspiration.

"Oh, my!" Susan finally managed to mutter.

"Oh, yes," Hunter agreed. Then he added, "Remind me to bring you coffee more often."

NESTLED IN A VALLEY between two snow-shrouded mountains, Green Acres Pavilion looked like something out of a fairy tale—an Oriental fantasy in an alpine setting.

"Wow," Susan said when it first came into view. She slowed down the car.

"And double wow," Hunter said, eyeing the facility from an architect's perspective. "It's enough to give both Frank Lloyd Wright and I. M. Pei nightmares. I wonder who designed it."

"Obviously, not someone you'd care to meet."

"I wouldn't say that. He probably has a great sense of humor. This thing," he said, gesturing to Green Acres, "is certainly a joke."

Susan laughed and speeded up the car again, heading for the parking lot in front of the eclectic structure. "What would you do to improve it?" she asked.

"Tear it down and start over from scratch," he replied without hesitation.

"Have you ever thought about getting back into design, Hunter?"

He looked at her with surprise, wondering if she'd read his mind. He'd worked briefly for an architectural firm right after his graduation from Georgia Tech. Then, when he and Susan became engaged, he'd resigned in order to accept Kenneth Brantley's offer of a position at his bank.

"As a matter of fact," he said slowly, "I'm already working on the design for a renovation project."

It was Susan's turn to be surprised. "You are?"

"It's only my sister's house," he said with a dismissive wave of his hand.

"That doesn't matter. The design itself is what's important. You always said so."

"You remember that after all this time?"

"I remember almost everything about you," she said so softly he could barely hear the words.

He felt a tightness in his throat. He didn't know what to say, so he said nothing.

Susan expertly guided the car into a parking space and turned off the ignition. "We're here."

The nervous excitement that Hunter had felt all morning took a quantum leap. "The moment of reckoning," he said.

"Hunter," she said hesitantly. "I hope you don't expect too much from this interview. I mean, Dr. Estep might not remember your case. He's probably treated hundreds of patients during his years of practice."

"I know," he said, recognizing that Susan was trying to prepare him for a possible disappointment. "He might not remember anything. After all, if he's a patient in a mental institution, there has to be a reason for it."

"Yes. And there's something else—they might not even let you see him."

"I thought about that. I'm prepared to lie if necessary, and tell them I'm a relative."

She frowned. "Isn't that awfully risky?"

"What can they do? Throw me in jail?"

"I just don't want you to get your hopes up too much," she said. "Seeing Dr. Estep isn't the most important thing in the world."

"Then why does it feel like it?"

They looked at each other in silence for long moments. Then Hunter leaned over to kiss Susan's cheek. "Thanks for caring about me."

She gave him a halfhearted smile. They got out of the car and walked silently to the front entrance of Green Acres Pavilion.

Unlike the garish exterior, the main lobby was tastefully decorated, more like a large private sitting room than an institution. On the left, just inside two sets of double doors, a receptionist sat at a desk behind a glass partition.

The woman was writing in a large ledger. Hunter waited a few moments and, when she still didn't seem to notice his presence, rapped on the glass. Startled, she looked up.

"Sorry," she said. "I didn't see you come in."

Hunter had to bend down slightly in order to speak through a circle cut out of the glass partition. "That's all right," he said, smiling at her.

The receptionist blinked and returned his smile. "May I help you?"

"I'm here to see a . . . patient. Dr. Wayne Estep."

"Are you a relative?"

Here we go, he thought. "Yes. I'm his cousin."

The woman wrote something on a notepad before looking at Hunter again. "Name, please?"

"Estep. Same as his."

"And your first name?"

Oh, hell. Why hadn't he thought this thing through properly? Should he claim his name was John Estep? Tom Estep? Bill or Joe or Bob Estep? Almost everyone had a relative with one of those names. But which one?

He took a deep breath. "Hunter Townsend. Hunter Townsend Estep."

The receptionist wrote on the pad again, then looked at Hunter. "Please have a seat in the lobby."

He hesitated. "Will I get to see him?"

"Someone will be with you in a moment."

Someone? Who was this someone? And would whoever it was take him to see Dr. Estep? He wanted to protest, to retract his lie about being a cousin, to tell her how important it was for him to see Wayne Estep. . . so important that his own sanity might depend on it.

But he had already been dismissed. The receptionist had talked briefly into a telephone and then returned her attention to the ledger. There was nothing else he could do but what she'd commanded—take a seat in the lobby.

"I blew it," he muttered to Susan after they'd arranged themselves side by side on a love seat. "Thanks to my stupidity, I'll never get in to see Estep." He didn't have to explain what he meant, because she'd been standing directly behind him and heard his entire conversation with the receptionist.

"You can't be sure of that," she said.

He shook his head. "Don't try to make me feel better."

They sat in silence.

"If they don't let you see Dr. Estep," she said finally, "maybe they'll let me."

Hunter stared at her. "Why would they do that?"

"I'd simply tell them the truth—that I'm Kenneth Brantley's stepdaughter. Maybe Dr. Estep remembers Kenneth's name, and will see me because of it."

"Suppose he did agree to see you. What good would that do?"

"Well, you could tell me what questions to ask him."

"Impossible," he said. "I don't even know myself what questions to—"

"Mr. Estep? Hunter Townsend Estep?"

Hunter looked up to see a white-clad male attendant staring down at him. *They probably sent a man so he could throw me out if I give him any trouble.*

"Uh, yes," Hunter said, bracing himself.

"Will you come with me?"

"Where to?" he asked suspiciously.

"To see your cousin."

Hunter blinked. He felt Susan's elbow nudge him in the ribs, and jumped to his feet. She quickly got up and stood beside him. "May I come, too?" she asked.

The attendant frowned.

"She's my wife," Hunter said.

"In that case, sure," the man said, breaking into a smile. "Follow me."

He led them onto an elevator and punched the button to the fourth floor. "Sorry to make you wait so long," he said. "Dr. Estep has a standing order for no visitors except family, so we had to clear it with him. You understand."

"Certainly," Hunter replied. He was amazed that his lie about being Dr. Estep's cousin had gained him entry. Didn't the man know the names of his own relatives? He wanted to look at Susan, but didn't dare.

When the elevator stopped on the fourth floor, the attendant led them down a long corridor. This was more hospital-like, more what Hunter had expected such a facility to be.

The attendant stopped outside a room, knocked on the door and opened it when a voice from inside said, "Come in."

Hunter took a deep breath and held it. He and Susan followed the attendant inside the room.

"Hunter! It's so good to see you again!"

He recognized the voice, if not the man who walked up to shake his hand. The voice belonged to Dr. Wayne Estep.

"You can leave us now, Raymond," Dr. Estep said to the attendant after he finally stopped shaking Hunter's hand. "Thanks for bringing my visitors."

Two years had certainly changed the good doctor, Hunter thought. The man he remembered was of medium height, thin and nervous, with thick brown hair and myopic brown eyes behind horn-rimmed glasses. This man was of medium height, but almost everything else was different.

His hair was pure white, unusual for a man somewhere in his mid-forties. That was the first thing Hunter noticed. The second was his dramatic weight gain. This Wayne Estep was almost roly-poly. His eyes were still brown and he still wore glasses, but these spectacles were tinted, aviator-style with metal rims.

"Well, Hunter, aren't you going to introduce me to this lovely young woman?" Dr. Estep asked.

"Uh . . . certainly." He made the introductions.

"Susan Willingham," Dr. Estep repeated, scratching his head. "I'm sure we haven't met. I'd never forget such a pretty face. But the name sounds familiar . . ."

"I'm Kenneth Brantley's stepdaughter," Susan said.

"Of course! Kenneth is the one who sent Hunter to me in the first place." He took Susan's hand and patted it. "You two were engaged."

"Yes," she said softly.

"I remember now. Kenneth told me to examine your young man tip to toe. He wanted Hunter fully vetted before he would allow him to marry his precious Susan." Dr. Estep chuckled. "How long have you two been married now?"

"We . . . we're not married," she said.

"No? Oh." He dropped her hand. "I . . ." He glanced at Hunter, then at Susan. "Well, those things happen sometimes, don't they?"

Susan nodded.

Dr. Estep nodded, too. Then he focused his attention on Hunter again. "It was very clever of you to claim you were my cousin, Hunter. You must have guessed that I refuse to see anyone except my family. Of course, you had no way of knowing that I don't have a cousin."

"You don't?" Hunter asked, surprised. "Then why did you agree to see me?"

"Because I recognized your name. Immediately."

Hunter's heart started beating faster. "Why would you recognize *my* name? You must have had hundreds of patients in your career . . . thousands."

"Yes," Dr. Estep said solemnly. "But as far as I know, you're the only one whose diagnosis I ever messed up so badly. Yours is a name I'll never forget."

Hunter held his breath.

The doctor turned to Susan. "I'm sure Hunter has told you what I told him—that he had an inoperable brain tumor with only about a year to live."

Susan's eyes widened. Her mouth opened and closed. She shook her head, seemingly unable to speak.

Dr. Estep shook his head, too, as if to clear his thoughts. "He came to see me just about the time my... sickness was starting. I was under a lot of pressure, you understand. Tremendous pressure... There was that messy divorce... and losing the children... too much work... too much alcohol and pills to put me to sleep at night... and then to get me going again in the morning... You know how that is."

The doctor was rambling now, and Hunter needed to put him back on track. "I never knew exactly how you happened to make the wrong diagnosis about me."

Dr. Estep suddenly jerked his head around, as if he'd been awakened, brought back from a trance. "I mixed up your test results with those of another patient, a man whose last name was Hunter," he said. "Didn't Kenneth tell you?"

Bingo!

Hunter clenched his fists, trying desperately to keep calm. "He may have said something..."

"I tried to get in touch with you as soon as I found out I'd inadvertently looked at the wrong test results when I made your diagnosis. It was only a few days later... certainly not more than a week... or was it two...?"

"I'm sure it wasn't long before you found out your mistake," Hunter said, prompting him.

"That's right. Not long at all. But I couldn't find you anywhere. So I called Kenneth. I was frantic by then. He told me not to worry. He said you were out of town, but that he would forward my letter to you containing the correct test results.''

Hunter was somewhat surprised by Estep's revelations. All this time, he'd thought that Brantley had engineered the doctor's misdiagnosis, but he hadn't. What he *had* done was take advantage of the physician's error in order to get rid of Hunter, which was bad enough.

There was still one more thing he needed to clear up. ''Did you ever talk with Brantley . . . I mean Kenneth, after that?''

''Oh, yes. He called me a few weeks later. He said you were still out of town . . . down in Florida somewhere, I think.''

''That's right. I was in the Keys. What did he say to you that time?''

Dr. Estep scratched his head for a moment while he thought. ''He told me the two of you had talked by phone after you got the good news, and that you were happy and relieved to learn there was nothing wrong with you. I wanted to call and apologize to you in person, but he said there was no need—that you understood about the pressure I'd been under and weren't angry.''

''And that's the last time you talked to him?''

''In person, it was. I understand that he came by to see me here once.''

''When was that? Was it about six months ago?''

''It could have been,'' Dr. Estep said, scratching his head once more. ''It probably was. But I was in no condition to see or talk to anybody back then. I tell you, Hunter, I was going through hell about that time.''

Hunter nodded sympathetically.

"But that's in the past," the doctor said. "All of it. You're alive and well, and I'm on the road to recovery." He laughed. "I just hope my misdiagnosis didn't inconvenience you too much."

Inconvenience? Hunter clenched his fists again. Up until then, he'd felt sorry for the man, but now he wanted to hit him. The doctor's stupid, senseless error had turned his entire life upside down... almost destroyed him... and Estep had the nerve to sit back now and refer to it as an *inconvenience?*

But of course the doctor didn't know—*couldn't* know—the living torment he'd put Hunter through. And the poor devil had already suffered enough himself.

Even so, Hunter couldn't bring himself to tell Estep he was forgiven. He compromised by holding out his hand instead. "I think we've already taken up enough of your time, Doctor," he said. "Perhaps too much."

"Nonsense," Dr. Estep said as they shook hands. "Time goes very slowly here."

"Yes. Well..." Hunter turned to Susan, and totally forgot what he'd been about to say.

She was completely still—as if she were a statue—and her face was almost as white as the remaining snow on the ground outside.

It was no wonder, Hunter thought. Despite the way he apparently dealt with other people, Brantley had been like a father to Susan, and she cared for him deeply. Hearing the truth about him must have come as a terrible blow to her.

Hunter moved close to her side and took her hand in his. It was like ice.

"Thank you for seeing us, Dr. Estep," Hunter said.

"Thank you for coming . . . cousin," the doctor replied with a last chuckle.

Susan said nothing.

Hunter gently led her out of the room and into the corridor. "Are you all right?" he asked.

She nodded. Hunter slipped his arm around her waist and led her down the corridor to the elevator, then through the lobby and out of the building. He wanted to give her time to get over her shock and sort out her feelings, so he didn't try to talk to her.

Susan still hadn't spoken when they reached her car, but her color was back to normal. "Are you feeling better now?" he asked.

She suddenly wheeled around, fury flashing from her green eyes. Hunter stepped back, feeling as if she'd just slapped him . . . or would very much like to.

"You bastard!" she said.

Chapter Fourteen

"Me?" Hunter said incredulously.

"Yes, you!" Susan shouted. She was so furious, she was shaking.

He shook his head. "You've got it wrong. I'm not the one who's the bad guy here."

"You wasted two years of your life... and my life, too. What does that make you?"

"I had no choice, Susan."

"The hell you didn't!"

"I thought I was dying, dammit!

"So you ran away," she said, clenching her fists in frustration. "You never had amnesia. You ran away because you were *scared!*"

"Of course I was scared. Any sane person would be if he was looking death in the face. But that's not why I left Atlanta."

"You were selfish," she accused. "Thinking only of yourself."

"That's not true!" he said angrily.

"Then why *did* you leave Atlanta?" She forced herself to say the rest of it. "Why did you leave me?"

He reached out to touch her then, but she brushed his hand away. When she did, the look he gave her was one of such pain that she almost threw her arms around him. It took all her willpower not to do it.

"Leaving you was the hardest thing I ever did," he said in a voice that cracked as he spoke. "I swear. It was like tearing out my own heart . . . a part of myself. But I knew I had to do it . . . for your sake."

"My sake?" she asked in disbelief.

"I was sure you'd insist on going through with the wedding if you knew the truth—or what I thought was the truth—about my illness. I couldn't allow you to make that sacrifice, so I decided to leave."

"You didn't simply leave, Hunter. You disappeared without a word or note of explanation. I was frantic at first. I thought you'd been kidnapped or killed. And later on, when I found out you were alive and well . . . that might have been even worse."

"I'm so sorry. I never intended any of that to happen," he said. "And I did *try* to write to you. I must have composed a dozen or more letters that wound up in the trash. There was nothing I could say that made any sense unless I told you I was dying, and that was the one thing I didn't want you to know."

"It would have been a blessing to know," she stated.

"I'm sorry, Susan," he said again. "Truly."

"I had a right to know! You owed me that much."

"I was trying to spare you."

"If you'd loved me enough, you would have—"

"No!" he shouted. "I loved you . . . still love you . . . more than life itself. That's why I wouldn't let you sacrifice yourself for me."

"Even if I wanted to be with you . . . more than life itself?"

Hunter nodded. "Yes. Even then. I knew I was facing months of pain, perhaps blindness. I knew I might become helpless. I couldn't let you suffer, too, because of me."

"Don't you think I suffered, anyway, Hunter?"

He blinked.

"Don't you think it still hurts me to think you didn't trust me?" she continued relentlessly.

"I don't understand what you mean," he said.

"Even though Dr. Estep told you that you only had a year to live, you still had that much time. A whole year, Hunter. That's twelve months...four seasons...close to four hundred days. We could have had all that time together if you'd trusted me enough to know I wouldn't fall apart on you when things were bad."

He shook his head. "I hadn't thought of it that way."

"Think about it," Susan said. She suddenly felt very tired, drained, so she opened the car door and slid into the driver's seat. She saw Hunter hesitate a moment before he walked around to the passenger side.

"Maybe you're right," he said, getting into the car. "Maybe I should have told you about my supposedly fatal illness two years ago. But I didn't."

She could feel his gaze on her. Finally, she turned to look at him.

"Can you ever forgive me?" he asked softly.

She wanted to. With all her heart, there was nothing she wanted more. She took a deep breath. "There's also the matter of your lies since you've been back."

"About having amnesia," he said.

"Yes."

"Look at it from my point of view, Susan. Would you have allowed me back in your life if I *hadn't* gone along with your mother in making that claim about losing my memory?''

"I might have."

He shook his head. "I doubt it. After recovering from the shock of seeing me again, you would have gone through with your wedding to Verner.''

"Did you ever consider telling me the truth? That sometimes works as a last resort.''

"You needn't be sarcastic. I feel bad enough, as it is.''

"The question still stands—why didn't you simply tell me the truth?'' she asked.

"Suppose I had told you the truth. Suppose I'd rushed up to you at your wedding and said, 'Susan, I thought I had a tumor and was dying two years ago, but I found out I didn't and I wasn't, so now I'm back.' Would you have believed such a story?''

"I don't know," she said truthfully. Then she thought about it some more. "Probably not.''

Hunter nodded. "My point exactly.''

"That reminds me of something else I've been meaning to ask. When did you find out that you didn't have a tumor, after all?''

"About a half a year ago." He gave a rueful laugh. "I became suspicious when I still felt fine six months after I was supposed to be dead. So I went to get a second opinion.''

"Why did you wait so long? I mean, why hadn't you been to see a doctor before then?''

"Why should I? Like I said, I felt fine. Besides, some of the time, I was in places where there were no doctors—Antarctica, for example.''

"I see. So you finally found out you were in good health, and then six months later, you came back to Atlanta.''

"Oh no you don't!" he said angrily. "You're not laying *that* guilt trip on me. As soon as I found out I was okay, the first thing I did—the very first—was try to get in touch with you."

"You did? I never knew..."

"Of course you never knew, because you weren't at home. You were 'on vacation with your fiancé.' Your damned *fiancé!* You were engaged again, to somebody else, only a year after I left. How would you have felt in my place, Susan?"

Horrified, all she could do was shake her head.

"I talked with the maid first, then with your beloved stepfather, Kenneth Brantley. He assured me he would relay the message that I was okay and had frantically been trying to get in touch with you. I assume you never got the message."

"No," Susan whispered. "I never got the message."

"I was in South America at the time—in a village that was barely large enough to attract the only doctor for hundreds of miles. There was nothing to do there, absolutely nothing. But I hung around for another week after I'd tried to call you, hoping against hope that you'd somehow return my call. You didn't."

Susan bit her lip, trying to hold back the tears. "I'm sorry, Hunter. That was a terrible mistake I made— becoming engaged."

"Why did you do it?"

"Loneliness, I suppose. And fear of being alone...I was so desolate after you left. Also, I imagine that subconsciously, I was trying to punish you for running off and leaving me. I know it's petty, but..." She shrugged.

"I understand," Hunter said, surprising her. "I've wanted to punish you, too. It's one of the reasons I came back."

She managed a weak smile. "You mean you didn't come back to marry me?"

"Not at first," he replied in all seriousness. "I wanted to embarrass you—and your stepfather—by disrupting your wedding ceremony. That's all I had in mind, until the amnesia thing came up. I latched on to that idea as a means of weaseling my way back into your life."

She suddenly understood a lot of things. "You used me to help you find out what part Kenneth played in your false diagnosis of a brain tumor." It was a statement, not a question.

"Yes," he admitted. "I thought he had engineered the whole thing in order to get rid of me."

Even though she could understand the reasons behind his duplicity, she still hurt.

"But then I fell in love with you again," Hunter said. "Or found out I loved you still. I'm not sure I ever stopped loving you."

That was the second time he'd mentioned love. Or was it the third? She took a deep breath.

"I love you, too, Hunter," she finally admitted. When he made a move to touch her, she held up her hand to stop him. "But I'm not sure we both agree on what love means."

"How can you say that?"

"It seems to me that you think love means only sharing the good times, not the bad. Love means much more than that to me."

"It does to me, too," he protested.

"Are you sure? What if it was the other way around, Hunter? What if I was the one who became ill? Would you expect me to go off by myself and face it alone?"

"Of course not!"

"Why not? It's what you did."

"That was different."

"Because you're a man? I didn't know you were so sexist. But then, I'm beginning to think I never knew you, not really. And if you think it would be my choice to have you conveniently crawl off to a hole somewhere to die, then you sure as hell don't know me!"

"You keep twisting things around. What I did two years ago was done for love, nothing else. I admit it was a mistake, but you shouldn't try to read something else into it."

He paused for breath before he continued. "You shouldn't keep shifting the blame, either. It was Kenneth Brantley—your precious stepfather—who's responsible for keeping us apart for two long years. Don't you fault him at all?"

"Of course I do. What Kenneth did was unbelievably cruel, heartless. There's no defense for it. But don't you forget one important thing, Hunter."

"What?"

"It wouldn't have happened . . . it couldn't have happened . . . if you hadn't run away in the first place."

NEITHER OF THEM spoke much on the drive back to Atlanta, and what they did say related to impersonal things—the weather, road conditions and such. Hunter tried to think of something to say, some way to reach Susan, but couldn't come up with anything that might change her way of thinking.

She couldn't seem to forget what she considered his unforgivable sin of running out on her two years ago. Yet, she was able to dismiss her stepfather's underhanded betrayal with only a few words. It didn't seem fair.

They were at an impasse.

Hunter prayed it was a temporary one. He certainly wasn't giving up on their relationship, not now that they'd found each other again, fallen in love with each other again.

Susan was right about one thing. He should never have run away from her two years ago. He wouldn't make that same mistake again, He wouldn't give her up a second time without a fight.

However, now wasn't the time to make that fight. First, he'd give her a chance to absorb all that she had learned today. And after she had, he'd allow her still more time—time for her own good judgment and sense of fair play to kick in.

Hunter was surprised when he looked out the car window and saw they were already in the suburbs of Atlanta. He'd been so lost in his thoughts that he hadn't noticed their progress. Now he needed to make a decision about where to go for the night. Should he try to connive his way into Susan's home again or go to his hotel?

The decision he'd already made—to give Susan time to think—finally decided the issue. She could do her thinking better without him around.

"Isn't the Doubletree Hotel somewhere around here?" he asked, pretending not to know.

She glanced at him with surprise. "It's the next exit."

"Will you drop me off there?"

"You're going to check into a hotel?"

"I have to stay somewhere. I've heard the Double-tree's nice." He should know. Except for the past three nights, he'd been staying at the hotel for a week, and still had a room waiting for him there.

"I thought there were no rooms available anywhere in Atlanta," Susan said slowly, bringing up another of his lies.

She looked at him again and he shook his head. He saw her sharp intake of breath. "I see," she said.

They didn't speak until she pulled the car to a stop in front of the Doubletree Hotel. "What are you go-ing to do now?" she asked.

"I'm going to try to set up a meeting with Brantley. I thought I'd call your mother to see if she'd arrange it . . . if you have no objection."

Susan shrugged. "She's free to make her own deci-sions." She absentmindedly twisted the leather grip on the steering wheel. "Are you planning to confront Kenneth with what you learned from Dr. Estep?"

"Yes."

"What good will it do?"

"None, perhaps. But it'll be good for my soul." He hesitated a moment. "I hope you'll be at the meeting, too. Unless you'd rather not."

"I . . . I'm not sure."

"I'll let you know what time we set it for. Just in case," Hunter said.

Susan nodded, but didn't promise anything.

A uniformed attendant helped Hunter take all his belongings from Susan's car and load them onto a cart. Hunter walked around to her door before fol-lowing the man inside the hotel. He leaned over to speak to her and she rolled down the window.

"I know you have a lot of things to think about," he said. "But I hope you'll remember this. I loved you two years ago, I love you now and I'll love you fifty years from now... or even longer. Promise me you won't forget that?"

They gazed into each other's eyes for a long time. "I promise," she whispered. Then she rolled up the car window and drove away.

Hunter strode into the hotel. He made a brief stop at the desk to pick up his key, then took an elevator to his room. After the attendant deposited his belongings and left, Hunter went to the phone to call Susan's mother.

"Hunter!" Mrs. Brantley said as soon as he identified himself. "Are you and Susan back from Dahlonega already?"

She sounded disappointed. "Yes," he said. "Susan dropped me off at the hotel just a few minutes ago."

"You mean she's not with you?"

That was definitely disappointment he heard in Mrs. Brantley's voice. "I think she's on her way home. Did you want to get in touch with her?"

"Not necessarily. Did you two have a fight? Is that why you came back so soon?"

"A fight?" he repeated. He started to deny it, but realized that he owed Mrs. Brantley the truth. "Well... sort of."

She sighed. "That's too bad. I was hoping you and Susan, being off alone together might..." She sighed again. "Never mind."

Hunter was thankful that Susan's mother didn't know—couldn't possibly know—the things that he'd done with her daughter last night and this morning while they were off alone together *before* they had the fight.

He knew Mrs. Brantley was dying to be told what the fight had been about, and that was one thing he *could* tell her. In fact, it was something she needed to know before he asked her help.

"Actually," he said, "what Susan and I had was more of an argument than a fight."

"An argument?" her mother repeated.

"Yes. Mostly about the past...especially what happened two years ago...and why it happened."

He proceeded to tell her what they'd learned from Dr. Estep, as well as some of what they'd argued about afterward. He tried to be fair in describing the points that Susan had made, in addition to those he'd brought up.

"I'm so glad," Mrs. Brantley said when he finished.

"What?" Hunter asked, genuinely astonished.

"Not about everything that happened!" she added quickly. "That wretched doctor almost ruined your life, with Kenneth's help. But I'm relieved to know why you disappeared the way you did. I was certain— well, almost certain—you had a good reason. And indeed you did! You were being noble because you loved Susan so very much!"

Hunter sighed. "I wish she felt the same way you do."

"Give her time. She'll soon come around. Did you two part as friends or enemies?"

"At the end, we sort of reached an impasse. I told Susan that I was going to ask your help in setting up a meeting with her stepfather, if you'd agree to it."

"You know I will. But only if I'm allowed to be present."

"I'm going to confront him with everything I know," Hunter warned her.

"That's something I wouldn't miss for the world," Mrs. Brantley stated emphatically.

"Then you're invited. I asked Susan to come, too, if she felt like it. I don't know whether she will or not."

"Would you like me to talk to her?"

"No! I mean, not on my behalf. She has to make up her own mind. After she has time to think things over, I think…I hope…" He didn't finish the sentence. He couldn't.

"Susan can be stubborn, but she has common sense, too, when she chooses to use it. I'm sure she'll make the right decisions eventually."

"I hope so," he breathed, making it a prayer.

"There's something I want to tell you, Hunter. But you may have already guessed it," Mrs. Brantley said. "Our divorce—Kenneth's and mine—had something to do with that phone call you made when you first found out that you didn't have a brain tumor."

"I wondered about that," he admitted. "I thought it was strange that you learned about my call from the maid, rather than from your husband. I'm sorry that I was the reason for—"

"There were many reasons for our divorce. But the fact that Kenneth concealed your phone call and then lied about it was more or less the last straw. And even though he finally confessed under pressure that you'd called, he never told me about the false diagnosis."

Hunter gave a low whistle. "I'd say you were well rid of him, Mrs. B."

"And I'd agree with you, Hunter," she said with a laugh. "I'm only telling you this so you'll know the type of man you're dealing with. Forewarned is forearmed."

"Thank you. I'll remember."

"Good. Now, when would you like me to set up this meeting between you two?"

"Anytime is fine with me," Hunter said. "The sooner the better."

"I'll try to get in touch with Kenneth right after we hang up," Mrs. Brantley promised. "Give me your number and I'll call you back as soon as I've arranged a definite time."

Hunter gave her his number and they said goodbye. After a moment, he walked to the window and gazed down on the late-afternoon winter scene fourteen stories below. The snow was melting rapidly now, he noticed. By tomorrow, all traces would probably be gone.

He felt suffused with warmth as he recalled Susan standing in the new-fallen snow in her driveway, her cheeks rosy from the cold, eyes sparkling with enjoyment. The picture faded, replaced by the image of her face close up, only a kiss away from his as she lay in his arms this morning. Her green eyes held a secret message of love and desire, meant for him alone.

He closed his eyes, deliberately expelling the image. He'd had enough of dreams—two long years enough of them. Now he wanted the real thing. He wanted Susan herself, live and in person, right by his side. Where she belonged.

He could only hope she would come to the same conclusion. And soon.

The phone rang.

Hunter ran to answer it and almost fell when his bad ankle protested. "Hello," he said breathlessly.

"It's all set," Helen Brantley said. "Tomorrow evening at five-thirty at my house. Sorry I couldn't convince Kenneth to make it sooner."

"Five-thirty's fine," Hunter said, trying to convince himself that it was true. He'd hoped to meet earlier. "And thank you very, very much...for everything."

She laughed. "You're very, very welcome, Hunter. See you then."

Hunter hung up the phone and stared at it. Then he clenched his fists, feeling a wild excitement. "Yes!" he said. It was finally happening. The only other thing— besides Susan—that he'd dreamed about during those years of separation was actually going to take place.

He raised both fists in the air.

"Yes!"

SUSAN WAS RELIEVED when she heard the phone ring. She'd been wandering aimlessly through the house— pacing, actually—since she got home. She felt lost, misplaced, disoriented.

She missed Hunter.

Lifting the receiver, she took a deep breath before answering. "Hello."

"Hi. It's Hunter."

"Yes. I mean, I recognized your voice." What a stupid thing to say!

"I, uh, just got off the phone with your mother."

"How is she?" Susan asked before she could stop herself. The question had just popped out of her mouth.

"She's fine."

Hunter paused—probably waiting to hear what stupid question or comment she'd make next—but she kept her mouth clenched tightly.

"The meeting between your stepfather and me is all set," he finally said. "It's at five-thirty tomorrow evening, at your mother's house."

"That's good. I mean . . . if *you* think it is."

"I do," he said. "I think it's very good."

They were both talking like awkward strangers. This morning, lying in his arms after they'd just made love for the third time in a matter of hours, she wouldn't have believed it possible that they'd be so estranged now. Poles apart. But they were. It made her want to cry.

"You're all set then," she said, trying to sound cheerful.

"Yes. Well, I told you I'd let you know about the meeting. . . ."

He seemed to be waiting for her to say something again. But what? "Thank you," she said.

"Susan . . ."

"What?"

"I hope you'll be there."

"I don't know, Hunter. Still. I'll think about it."

"Please do."

They said goodbye then. As she started to hang up the phone, she thought she heard Hunter say something else. It was so low—almost a whisper—that she couldn't be sure, but she thought it sounded like, "I love you."

She quickly brought the receiver back to her ear, and heard only a dial tone. She was probably mistaken. What she'd thought she heard was probably only wishful thinking.

HUNTER PAID the driver and got out of the taxi. He took a couple of steps toward Susan's mother's home, then stopped to collect himself. This might not have been the most stressful day of his life, but it had to rank right up there.

Plus, it seemed sixty hours long. He'd been up at dawn after a fitful night's sleep. He took an early-morning walk in order to relax himself for the big day ahead. The weather was cold and crisp, and nobody else was on the jogging path to get in his way.

That part was great, but the day went steadily downhill from there. The walk didn't relax him as he'd hoped it would. If anything, it seemed to stimulate him, making him so edgy that he couldn't sit still, couldn't read and could barely eat. He paced his hotel room. He walked over to Perimeter Mall and made several circuits around both the interior floors. He walked back to the hotel and paced his room some more.

And so it went.

He must have picked up the phone to call Susan almost a dozen times, but had been able to resist dialing her number. He *had* to give her time alone, he kept telling himself. All the while, he kept hoping she would call him. But she hadn't.

Hunter squared his shoulders and started up the front steps; steps he'd climbed many times when he was dating Susan years ago. He wasn't intimidated by the house—a graceful Georgian design that he'd always admired. It was what was waiting for him inside the house that had kept him on edge all day.

He rang the doorbell, and was surprised when Helen Brantley opened the door herself. "What?" he said. "Is this the maid's night off?"

She laughed—a delightfully melodic sound much like her daughter's laugh. "Every night is maid's night off, Hunter," she said, taking his overcoat. "I don't have the staff I used to. And frankly, I like it better this way."

She looped her arm through his and led him toward one of his favorite rooms in the house, the family drawing room. "Kenneth is already here," she said. "But I didn't tell him that *you* were the other guest I was expecting for cocktails."

Hunter stopped walking. "You didn't?"

"Call me a coward."

"You're certainly not that. There has to be another reason."

"Well...I *did* want to see the expression on his face when you walked through the door."

"That's better," he said, nodding his head as they started walking again.

When they got to the drawing-room door, Hunter reached to open it. "Here we go," Mrs. Brantley whispered, giving him a wink as she preceded him through the door.

Taking a deep breath, Hunter followed her. He closed the door, and turned to face his longtime enemy.

"What's *he* doing here?" Kenneth Brantley asked, jumping to his feet.

"I invited him, of course," his ex-wife explained calmly. "He's my other guest."

"You know how I feel about him," Brantley said, shooting a malevolent glance at Hunter.

"Yes. And you know that I don't share your feelings," she retorted.

"I won't forget this, Helen."

"I'm sure you won't, Kenneth." She gave him a fleeting smile. "Now. Will you fix Hunter a drink?"

"No," Brantley replied curtly. He sat back down in his chair beside the fireplace.

"Very well. I'll do it myself. What would you like, Hunter?"

"Water, please." He wanted to keep a clear head.

Mrs. Brantley nodded and moved to the nearby serving cart, where she skillfully used silver tongs to put two ice cubes into a glass, then poured water from a crystal pitcher. She picked up a cocktail napkin and brought the glass to Hunter.

"Thank you," he said.

"You're welcome. Now, come have a seat by the fire."

Hunter followed her direction and sat in the chair opposite Brantley's. Susan's mother positioned herself on the sofa between the two chairs. Hunter could feel the other man's gaze trained on them as they moved.

"Is there a point to all this, Helen?" Brantley asked when everyone was seated.

"Well, yes, now that you ask. There most certainly is a point. Since it directly concerns Hunter, I'll let him have the floor." She turned to him with an encouraging smile.

Here we go, Hunter thought. He wished Susan were here, for moral support if nothing else. But she wasn't. "I talked with Dr. Estep yesterday," he said.

"Who?"

Hunter had to hand it to Brantley. The man didn't bat an eye. "Dr. Wayne Estep," Hunter said. "He's the physician you referred me to for a physical two years ago."

Brantley shook his head. "Never heard of him."

"Yes, you have, Kenneth," Mrs. Brantley said. "You used to go to him yourself."

Bless you, wonderful lady, Hunter thought. *I only wish your daughter was on my side the way you are.*

"You know how many doctors I go to, Helen," Brantley said. "I can't be expected to remember all their names."

"You should remember Dr. Estep's name," Hunter told him. "He said you came all the way to Dahlonega to visit him at Green Acres Pavilion a few months ago."

Brantley narrowed his eyes as he looked at Hunter. "What's your point?"

Hunter took a deep breath. "After Dr. Estep examined me two years ago, he told me that I had an inoperable brain tumor. He said I had only about a year to live. He was wrong, totally wrong. There was no tumor."

"Congratulations," Brantley said sarcastically.

"Dr. Estep discovered his error a short time later," Hunter continued, ignoring Brantley's comment. "He immediately tried to get in touch with me, but I'd left town by then. I'd gone off by myself to die."

"So?" Brantley said. "Do you expect me to shed tears over your little sob story?"

"No," Hunter replied. "But the point is—although Dr. Estep wasn't able to get in touch with me, he was able to reach you. He told you the whole story."

"That's preposterous!"

"You promised Dr. Estep that you'd find me right away and tell me about the error. You promised him that you'd let me know I wasn't going to die."

"How could I do that when I didn't even know where you were, myself?" Brantley asked. He turned to his ex-wife. "You remember. None of us knew where he'd run off to."

She shook her head. "The detective we hired found Hunter only a few weeks later. You could have told him then."

"Told him!" Brantley shouted, finally showing signs of unraveling. "There was nothing for me to tell! Surely you don't believe this outrageous garbage."

"I'm afraid I do believe it, Kenneth. All of it."

"You can't! It's—"

"And what about the time I talked to you eighteen months later?" Hunter asked, interrupting Brantley. "You promised me you'd tell Susan I wanted to talk to her. You never told her."

"Don't try to deny that you spoke to him then, Kenneth," Mrs. Brantley said. "I know you did."

"Of course I talked to him! But nothing was said about a tumor...or dying...any of it. Townsend was half-drunk when he called. He probably doesn't even remember."

"I remember," Hunter said, directing his comments to Mrs. Brantley. "And I hadn't had anything to drink. I was still in the doctor's office after getting a second medical opinion when I called."

She nodded.

"Don't listen to him!" Brantley shouted, jumping to his feet. "He's making all of this up."

Hunter got up, too. "What about the things Dr. Estep admitted to me?"

Brantley snorted. "The man's in a mental hospital. He's crazy."

"No," Hunter said. "He had a breakdown, but he's not crazy. Not even close."

"If Estep isn't crazy, then you're lying. Take your choice." Brantley turned to his ex-wife again. "It's a pack of lies. All of it."

"No, it isn't."

Hunter wheeled around at the sound of the voice coming from behind him—Susan's voice. She was standing just inside the room. Michael Verner was with her.

Hunter hadn't heard them come into the room. Obviously, Brantley hadn't heard them, either, because his mouth was open. Even Mrs. Brantley's eyes were wide with surprise as Susan moved closer and Verner followed.

"Dr. Estep isn't crazy, and Hunter isn't lying," Susan stated emphatically.

"Susan," her stepfather said, finding his voice. "What are you doing here?"

"Hunter invited me," she replied simply.

She gave Hunter a fleeting, tentative smile. He would have been overjoyed to see her, overjoyed that she'd come, if Verner hadn't been with her. Had the two of them gotten back together? He clenched his fists in frustration.

"I asked Michael to come along, too," Susan continued. "I thought he should be better acquainted with the man who's trying to bring about a merger of their two banks."

"What?" Hunter asked.

"What?" Mrs. Brantley echoed.

"Isn't that right, Kenneth?" Susan said.

Her stepfather frowned at her. "This is neither the time nor the place—"

"You're right, of course," she agreed, interrupting him. "You and Michael will have plenty of time to discuss business later. And right now, we have other business at hand."

Hunter was watching her with admiration. *Damn, but he was proud of her—marching in here the way she had, standing up to her stepfather the way she was doing... She was magnificent!*

While he was watching her, Susan turned to look at him. Gazing directly into his eyes, she slowly lifted her hand to her cheek. The gesture struck Hunter as rather unusual.

It took him a few seconds to figure out why she'd done it. When he did, he stopped breathing. He blinked his eyes, not daring to believe that what he was seeing was really true.

The hand she held up to her cheek was her left hand. And she was wearing a ring on her third finger. It was an engagement ring—*his* engagement ring—the same one he'd given her on a star-filled, love-filled night over two years ago!

Hunter couldn't help it. He broke into a silly grin.

Susan lifted her head defiantly, as if to challenge him. Her eyes were unusually bright. He continued to grin.

After long moments, she lowered her hand and returned her attention to her stepfather. "Let's discuss the matter of what you did to Hunter."

"I did nothing," Brantley said.

"For more than a year, you deliberately let him go on believing he was dying. You call that nothing? Can you grasp—do you have any concept of how unbelievably cruel that was?"

"I didn't..."

"Yes, you did. I was present when Hunter talked to Dr. Estep at Green Acres. I heard every word the doctor said. He told you about the mix-up less than a week after it happened. You kept it a secret from everyone, including me... but especially including Hunter."

Brantley sneered. "You're conveniently forgetting that there was no way I could tell Townsend anything. He'd already run out on you!"

"That's the same argument I used yesterday," Susan said. "I was wrong."

"Are you denying that he left you—practically at the altar—without a word of explanation?"

"No. But what's truly important is the *reason* he left." She paused only long enough to send Hunter a loving glance, then turned once more to her stepfather.

"He left because he loved me enough to give me up when he thought he'd be a burden. What he did was noble... truly noble and self-sacrificing. I wonder if many people would have the strength of character to make such a sacrifice. I wonder if *I'd* have such strength... such courage."

She looked at Hunter again. "I didn't fully understand all of that yesterday. But I do now. That's why I'm here."

She held out her hand and Hunter took it in his. He squeezed gently.

"It's my turn to prove myself to him," Susan said. "I have to prove that I can be trusted to take care of our love, that I'll protect it, and him, just as he protected me."

Hunter swallowed around the huge lump in his throat. He squeezed Susan's hand again, trying to tell her with his touch how very much he loved her. She squeezed back, telling him with her touch and with her eyes that she returned his love.

"Susan, don't do this!" Brantley pleaded.

She reluctantly tore her gaze away from Hunter's. "Do what?"

"Throw your entire life away!" Brantley said. "You can't—"

"I've already made my decision . . . I think," she added, looking at Hunter.

He grinned. "I have witnesses."

"Everything I did was for you," Brantley said. "I've been like a father to you . . . I've always taken care of you . . ."

"No!" Susan said.

Brantley stepped back as if she'd slapped him.

"You're forgetting what you put Hunter through. What you did to him was inexcusable." She took a deep breath, and slipped her arm around Hunter's waist. "And what you do to him . . . you do to me."

There was complete silence in the room.

Nobody moved.

Nobody spoke.

Then Helen Willingham Brantley clapped her hands together once . . . twice . . . a third time.

"Bravo!" she said.

Epilogue

The wedding at the Cathedral of St. Phillip's was lovely, everything Susan had ever dreamed. What's more, it went off exactly as they'd planned—precisely on time and with no surprises. Thank God.

Susan's uncle gave her away, and Hunter's brother-in-law was best man. Her girlhood friend, Nancy Wages, performed the ceremony. Susan insisted that the bridesmaids wear the same dresses they'd bought for her aborted wedding to Michael.

The Piedmont Driving Club was a perfect site for the reception, as expected. And this time, they had a receiving line. It seemed to go on forever. Susan didn't mind it, but she could tell that Hunter was growing more antsy by the moment.

Also, she could have done without all the people who leaned over and whispered to her confidentially, "This proves that the third time is a charm."

Finally, the line dwindled and dried up, which meant that everybody had been received. After that, champagne was popped, toasts were drunk, best wishes and kisses were exchanged.

Now, as the orchestra started playing "When I Fall In Love," Hunter stepped forward to claim her for their first dance as husband and wife. He smiled and held out his hand to her. She smiled back and placed her hand in his.

Then she was in his arms. She heard their guests applaud as he whirled her in a circle. Susan wondered if anyone had ever been as happy as she was at this very moment.

Hunter brought his head close to hers and whispered in her ear, "Alone at last!"

"Alone?" she said with a laugh. "With hundreds of people surrounding us? Watching us while we dance?"

"Ah," he said. "But they don't know what we're saying to each other."

"That's true," she said with surprise. "They can see us but they can't hear us."

"Exactly. Do you want to talk dirty?"

Susan laughed again. "Actually, no. But it's comforting to know I could if I wanted to."

"I love you, Mrs. Townsend."

Her heart skipped a beat, then started racing wildly. "That's the first time anyone has ever called me by that name."

"Do you like it?"

"Very much." She lifted an eyebrow. "And I especially like all that it entails."

"It's a good thing you like your new name," he said, lifting his own eyebrow. "You'll have it for a long, long time... and all that it entails."

They both laughed. Then he whirled them in an exhilarating spin that left her breathless. Their guests applauded again.

"Show-off," she said softly when she was able to talk.

"Absolutely. I'm proud to show off my beautiful bride to the whole world," he said, twisting her comment around. "But speaking of showing you off reminds me of something."

"What?"

"You look spectacular in your wedding dress, but it looks a little different than I remembered from your wedding to Verner."

"It should. It's not the same dress."

"Good," he said. "I'm glad you bought a new one."

"It's not a new one, either."

He gave her a puzzled look.

"It's the dress I planned to wear at our wedding—yours and mine—two years ago."

Hunter blinked. "You kept it all this time?"

"Not me. I was all for ripping it to shreds," she answered truthfully. "My mother saved it."

"I owe that woman a lot more than I can ever repay," he said somberly. Then he brightened. "Is it okay with you if I'm in love with your mother?"

"I'm not the jealous type," she replied with a light laugh.

"I *am* the jealous type," Hunter said. "And right now I see your ex-fiancé standing over there practically drooling while he waits for his chance to dance with you."

"Michael? You have no reason to be jealous of him."

"Haven't you heard that love is unreasonable as well as blind?"

"Besides," Susan continued, "he's practically engaged to Nancy Wages."

"Nancy Wages?" Hunter repeated incredulously. "The minister?"

Susan nodded. "When I broke my engagement to Michael, I suggested to him that he talk to someone with a sympathetic ear, like Nancy. He took my advice and they hit it off right away. Nancy told me they're almost ready to set a date."

"Well, what do you know?" Hunter said, shaking his head. "I guess he's not such a bad guy, after all."

Susan nodded her agreement. "He certainly saved Kenneth's skin."

After having his eyes opened to Kenneth Brantley's true character, Michael had immediately called a halt to their merger negotiations. He'd sent in a team of independent auditors, who had found widespread mismanagement at Kenneth's bank, including the reckless loan practices Hunter had discovered years before.

Kenneth's bank was on the very brink of going under.

Instead of letting that happen, Michael had made a generous offer to take it over himself. Kenneth would be forced out, of course, but he'd be able to save face. More importantly, the bank's investors wouldn't be hurt.

Kenneth had jumped at Michael's offer, then had immediately gone away on an extended vacation.

"Have you still not heard from Brantley?" Hunter asked Susan.

She shook her head. "Nobody has. But I imagine he'll resurface eventually, when he thinks everyone has forgotten."

"When he does," Hunter began tentatively, "will you forgive him? He does love you, you know, as much as he's capable of love."

"I'm not sure," she replied. "Perhaps in time, I will. But I'm positive about one thing. I'll never forget what he did to you. To us."

"Did I tell you I love you very, very much?" he whispered.

"A few times," she whispered back, loving him so much it was almost a physical ache inside her. She swallowed. "Do you mind that we're not taking our honeymoon on that island you know in the South Pacific?"

She had persuaded him to finish the renovation on his sister's house rather than take a long trip now. The house would serve as a showcase for his talent and would bring in additional clients, she hoped...they both hoped. It would start him again on the career he'd always wanted—the work he was meant to do.

He shook his head. "We'll have plenty of time for that later. We have a whole lifetime."

He pulled her closer, kissing her forehead. Their audience applauded yet again.

He kissed her cheek. The audience clapped louder.

He kissed her lips. The audience went wild.

"Hunter!" she whispered fiercely. "Stop it!"

"It's okay. We're married."

"Still..."

"You're blushing!"

"Just wait until I get you alone," she threatened.

He wiggled his eyebrows. "I am waiting...and none too patiently, I might add."

Susan laughed with sheer happiness. "What am I going to do with you?"

"Love me, I hope," he replied seriously. "For an eternity."

"That's a given," she said softly, sliding her arms around his neck and pulling his head down to kiss him this time.

They stopped dancing entirely, giving themselves over to the mutual pleasure of kissing each other senseless.

Their dignified audience stomped and yelled, expressing its approval.

IT'S A BABY BOOM!

NEW ARRIVALS

We're expecting—again! Join us for a reprisal of the New Arrivals promotion, in which special American Romance authors invite you to read about equally special heroines—all of whom are on a nine-month adventure! We expect each mom-to-be will find the man of her dreams—and a daddy in the bargain!

Watch for the newest arrival!

#600 ANGEL'S BABY
by Pamela Browning
September 1995

Take 4 bestselling love stories FREE

Plus get a FREE surprise gift!

Special Limited-time Offer

Mail to Harlequin Reader Service®

3010 Walden Avenue
P.O. Box 1867
Buffalo, N.Y. 14269-1867

YES! Please send me 4 free Harlequin American Romance® novels and my free surprise gift. Then send me 4 brand-new novels every month, which I will receive months before they appear in bookstores. Bill me at the low price of $2.89 each plus 25¢ delivery and applicable sales tax, if any.* That's the complete price and a savings of over 10% off the cover prices—quite a bargain! I understand that accepting the books and gift places me under no obligation ever to buy any books. I can always return a shipment and cancel at any time. Even if I never buy another book from Harlequin, the 4 free books and the surprise gift are mine to keep forever.

154 BPA ANRL

Name   (PLEASE PRINT)

Address   Apt. No.

City   State   Zip

This offer is limited to one order per household and not valid to present Harlequin American Romance® subscribers. *Terms and prices are subject to change without notice. Sales tax applicable in N.Y.

UAM-295   ©1990 Harlequin Enterprises Limited

HARLEQUIN®

AMERICAN ✦ ROMANCE®
®

You asked for it…You got it! More MEN!

MORE
THAN
MEN

We're thrilled to bring you another special edition of the
popular MORE THAN MEN series.

Like those who have come before him. Ambrose Carpenter
is more than tall, dark and hansome. All of those men have
extraordinary powers that made them "more than men."
But whether they are able to grant you three wishes,
or live forever, make no mistake—their greatest, most
extraordinary power is of seduction.

So make a date with Ambrose Carpenter in…

#599 THE BABY MAKER
by Jule McBride
September 1995

MTM4

As a Privileged Woman,
you'll be entitled to all these Free Benefits. And Free Gifts, too.

To thank you for buying our books, we've designed an exclusive FREE program called *PAGES & PRIVILEGES*™. You can enroll with just one Proof of Purchase, and get the kind of luxuries that, until now, you could only read about.

Big HOTEL DISCOUNTS

A privileged woman stays in the finest hotels. And so can you—at up to 60% off! Imagine standing in a hotel check-in line and watching as the guest in front of you pays $150 for the same room that's only costing you $60. Your *Pages & Privileges* discounts are good at Sheraton, Marriott, Best Western, Hyatt and thousands of other fine hotels all over the U.S., Canada and Europe.

Free DISCOUNT TRAVEL SERVICE

A privileged woman is always jetting to romantic places. When you fly, just make one phone call for the lowest published airfare at time of booking—or double the difference back! PLUS—

you'll get a $25 voucher to use the first time you book a flight AND 5% cash back on every ticket you buy thereafter through the travel service!

FREE GIFTS!

A privileged woman is always getting wonderful gifts.
Luxuriate in rich fragrances that will stir your senses (and his). This gift-boxed assortment of fine perfumes includes three popular scents, each in a beautiful designer bottle. <u>Truly Lace</u>...This luxurious fragrance unveils your sensuous side. L'Effleur...discover the romance of the Victorian era with this soft floral. <u>Muguet des bois</u>...a single note floral of singular beauty.

YOURS FREE!

$50 VALUE

FREE INSIDER TIPS LETTER

A privileged woman is always informed. And you'll be, too, with our free letter full of fascinating information and sneak previews of upcoming books.

MORE GREAT GIFTS & BENEFITS TO COME

A privileged woman always has a lot to look forward to. And so will you. You get all these wonderful FREE gifts and benefits now with only one purchase...and there are no additional purchases required. However, each additional retail purchase of Harlequin and Silhouette books brings you a step closer to even more great FREE benefits like half-price movie tickets... and even more FREE gifts.

L'Effleur...This basketful of romance lets you discover L'Effleur from head to toe, heart to home.

Truly Lace...
A basket spun with the sensuous luxuries of Truly Lace, including Dusting Powder in a reusable satin and lace covered box.

Complete the Enrollment Form in the front of this book and mail it with this Proof of Purchase.

PROOF OF PURCHASE
Offer expires October 31, 1996

HAR-PP4